Boring

RIVER OF SECRETS

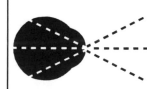

This Large Print Book carries the
Seal of Approval of N.A.V.H.

RIVER OF SECRETS

LYNETTE EASON

THORNDIKE PRESS
A part of Gale, Cengage Learning

GALE
CENGAGE Learning·

Detroit • New York • San Francisco • New Haven, Conn • Waterville, Maine • London

GALE
CENGAGE Learning˙

Thorndike Press® Large Print Christian Fiction.
The text of this Large Print edition is unabridged.
Other aspects of the book may vary from the original edition.
Set in 16 pt. Plantin.
Printed on permanent paper.

LIBRARY OF CONGRESS CATALOGING-IN-PUBLICATION DATA

Eason, Lynette.
    River of secrets / by Lynette Eason. — Large print ed.
        p. cm. — (Thorndike Press large print Christian fiction)
    Originally published: New York : Steeple Hill, 2008.
    ISBN-13: 978-1-4104-1491-5 (alk. paper)
    ISBN-10: 1-4104-1491-4 (alk. paper)
    1. Large type books. I. Title.
PS3605.A79R58 2009
813'.6—dc22   2008056115

Published in 2009 by arrangement with Harlequin Books S.A.

Printed in the United States of America
1 2 3 4 5 6 7 13 12 11 10 09

For God sees not as man sees, for man looks at the outward appearance, but the Lord looks at the heart.

— 1 *Samuel* 16:7

Dedicated to Jesus Christ

ACKNOWLEDGMENTS

I've come to the conclusion that it's impossible to say thank you to everyone. I'm so blessed by the many people God has placed in my life to encourage me, support me and love me.

I would like to say thanks again to my husband, Jack. You're awesome and I love you. 'Nuff said.

My children . . . Lauryn and Will, you guys are the best. I don't deserve you, but I love you beyond words.

Mom, Dad and Lane, thanks for all the writing time you provide. There's no way I could do it without you.

Bill and Diane, my in-laws, thanks for giving me Jack.

My writing buddy, Ginny Aiken, thanks for all the fun conversations and brainstorming sessions!

Thanks, Dee, for endorsing *Lethal Deception* — You rock!

And my editor, Emily Rodmell, I didn't forget you this time! Thanks for making my books shine.

And to all of you who buy my books, I can never tell you what it means to know you like them! Thank you!

And, of course, thank you, Jesus, for giving me the opportunity to share my love for you through my love of writing.

ONE

"We need help, Amy."

Amy Graham remembered the director of the Amazon orphanage's words. Ever since her mother had been arrested and sent to prison, Amy had felt as if she were foundering, seeking God's plan for a life that been flung off course. So she'd told Anna Freeman that she'd be glad to come to Brazil to put her RN training to work.

Now she was here, in Tefe, Brazil, not only to help nurse some sick people back to health, but to find family she'd just learned may exist. Excitement warred with fear of the unknown. What would they be like? Would they be interested in meeting her? She shivered, praying God would lead her, show her the direction to take with her search.

She looked around her and grabbed a stethoscope from the wall next to her. In the meantime, she'd do her best to help these poor, suffering people recover.

The sparse medical staff busied themselves rushing from one patient to another. A low moan sounded to her right. She stepped around the curtain and saw a man thrashing and kicking his covers on the cot.

Quickly, she moved next to him and grabbed the cloth from the water bowl that had been placed on the little stand next to the bed. Wishing the liquid was cooler, she worked with what she had and placed the rag on his forehead, watching his eyes twitch under his lids.

Obviously dreaming, his head tossed back and forth as he muttered under his breath. Amy slid the cloth over the scars that began on the left side of his face, covered his ear, then inched down the side of his neck to disappear into the collar of his shirt. Compassion filled her. He'd been in a serious fire.

"No!"

Amy jumped, her heart pounding, and scrambled backward. The patient's eyes remained clenched tightly against whatever tormented him; he continued to mutter unintelligibly.

She slid back to his side, shook his shoulder and tried to soothe him. "Hey, it's okay, wake up." Amy knew as long as his fever stayed this high, he wouldn't understand a word she said. Trembling, he quivered with the effort to fight the illness. She grabbed his chart to see when he'd last been given medication. Four hours ago. His name was Juan.

"Is everything all right?"

Amy looked up to see the woman whose call had brought her here. Anna, looking concerned, peered around the curtain.

Amy nodded. "He's having a nightmare." She gestured with the chart. "His fever's back up and he needs more meds. It's been a little over four hours."

Weariness oozing from her like a living thing, Anna took the chart, looked at it and made a notation. "Let me get something from one of the nurses. All the medicine is kept on a rolling medicine cart and is labeled if you need to get something. But I'll go ahead and get his for you. Be right back." A moment later, she returned with a filled syringe. Some of the really bad cases, such as Juan, had IVs.

Inserting the needle in the IV port, Anna said, "I'm not a nurse, but I've been trained to give injections in this emergency situation, just in case you were wondering." She nodded to the patient. "Juan is special. Why don't you stick with him as much as possible? When he's sleeping peacefully, you can work with some of the children. But I think it would really help him to have someone here."

Amy looked back at the poor man. "What's so special about him?"

"He's an amnesiac. The most we could figure out is that he survived some horrific fire, got conked on the head, woke up from an eleven-month coma and can't remember a thing about himself."

Amy gasped. "That's awful."

"No kidding. The whole time he was in the coma, Dr. Bennett, our mission doctor, worked with him tirelessly. Physical therapy, daily massages, turning him almost hourly so he wouldn't get bedsores. He became the staff's special project. Dr. Bennett even found someone to cover for him at the mission and moved into the hospital for the duration. A plastic surgeon buddy from the U.S. flew in to do some skin grafts. Thankfully, the burns on his face weren't as bad as originally believed, so the grafts were mostly successful. The scars will continue to fade with time, although they'll never be completely gone. His torso took the brunt of the burns. When he finally woke up, Juan had to learn how to walk again, feed himself, toilet himself. Everything. Daily, he went through a strenuous workout regimen with weights. I've never seen anyone so determined to get better. It's absolutely amazing he's come this far in a year and a half. In fact, they've posted more flyers around the town asking if anyone recognizes him now. He looks a lot different than he did a year ago."

"Juan — John? As in John Doe? And you don't know where he's from?"

"No. We know he's an American simply because of his accent. But he speaks perfect Portuguese. He actually woke up speaking that and didn't realize he could speak English until one day an American tourist was in the bed next to him. Lucas walked in on them carrying on a conversation in English."

"Why didn't they fly him back to America if they knew he was American?"

"Where would they fly him *to?* America's a pretty big country. Lucas figured if he kept him here, someone might come looking for him."

"So, how did he end up in the hospital?"

"He just showed up on the doorstep one day as close to death as you can get without actually dying. Someone had to have helped him get there, but obviously wanted to remain anonymous. Lucas answered the knock on the door, found him and immediately got to work on him. If it wasn't for Lucas . . ."

A scruffy, red-tinged beard covered most of the lower part of Juan's face, the part that could still grow hair. There were a few bald patches. She wondered what color his eyes were. "How long has he been this sick?"

"Almost three days. The dengue-fever outbreak hit him hard. It doesn't help that his lungs were weak to begin with. He had inhaled a lot of smoke from the fire and was on oxygen for a long time. Now this upper-respiratory thing. Lucas said his breathing's okay right now, but if he gets worse, we'll have to put him on oxygen. In addition, he often has awful nightmares. They plague him, but he can't remember what they are when he wakes up. I wish we had a good psychiatrist that could help him, but out here, there's really not anyone. Dr. Bennett offered to fly one in for him, but Juan refused." Anna sighed, folded her papers to stick into the pocket of her white lab coat. "I'll be back. I've got to check on the little ones."

Amy grabbed the wet cloth once again. The medication seemed to be working; he was calmer, resting better, although he still frowned in his sleep. Dipping the cloth, she wrung it out as she studied his face.

He looked familiar, yet she knew she'd never seen him before. She swiped the rag across his forehead, down his scarred left arm to his hand. No ring, not even a line across his finger. Raised welts, healed burns, crisscrossed the back of his hand. She turned it over. His palm was free of scars, but calloused from hard work. She ran the cloth back up to his neck over features that shouted strength, determination and stubbornness. Those traits had obviously served him well, kept him alive. Now she would do what she could to make him comfortable and pray for his healing.

She was back.

Juan coughed, but the burning, smothering sensation had disappeared. He felt sweaty and cool. Terror suddenly struck him. How long had he been asleep? Would he be able to move? Afraid to try, he wondered how much of his life he'd lost this time. What if he had to start all over again?

That familiar feminine voice washed over him, soothing him, compelling him to come out of the darkness that pressed onto him. "Hey there, Juan. We need you to wake up and start eating something."

A cool cloth on his forehead brought some relief.

When she bent over him, Juan got a whiff of lavender soap, a scent that he'd come to associate with her presence. Often he knew she was there even before she spoke. Mustering all of his nerve, he pried open eyes that wanted to stay shut — and looked full into her compassionate blue gaze. A messy, dark blond pony tail trailed over her right shoulder, soft tendrils escaping to frame her face. Smooth skin devoid of makeup stretched tight over delicate, high cheekbones.

A face to match the voice that brought him comfort. His nurse? He clenched his fist and breathed a sigh of relief. His muscles worked this time. He was okay. Memory came back; part of it, anyway. Dengue. Upper-respiratory infection. Fever, cough.

She smiled revealing perfectly straight white teeth. "Glad you're back with us. Would you like a drink of water?"

Juan let her smile wrap itself around his heart. "Please," he rasped.

Something rattled behind him, and she spoke again. "We've got ice water. Romero got the freezer working again and the new one arrived two days ago. Your fever is down, but just take a few tiny sips of the water, okay? Your body needs to recover."

"Yeah, I'm having flashes of déjà vu." He cleared his throat, used a shaky hand to place the cup against dry lips and sipped. "Thank you."

The effort exhausted him. Great. Back to square one. "What's your name?"

"Amy."

Pretty lady, pretty name. "Nice to meet you, Amy, I'm Juan. So, when can I get up and get back to my rooms?"

Amy shrugged. "As soon as you feel like you can, I suppose. I suggest you stay put for a couple more days."

Staying put wasn't an option. Juan had had enough of being sick and lying flat on his back. He shifted, groaned and sat up. Dizziness assailed him. He gasped at how weak he felt and flopped back onto the pillow.

Amy smiled a knowing, I-told-you-so smile, but said nothing. Juan grimaced and said, "I think I'll take a nap."

"I think that's a splendid idea." She reached out a steady hand to feel his forehead and Juan fell asleep to the touch of Amy's fingers trailing down his cheek.

Two days later, Amy took on the job of opening the cardboard boxes filled with medications that lay scattered around her feet. They'd arrived compliments of Lucas Bennett, who'd come from the medical mission to make the delivery and check on patients.

She thought about everything as she stocked the medicine carts. She'd had little sleep in the time she'd been here, but that didn't seem to matter. Especially when it came to Juan. He'd become as special to her as Anna had said he was. From feeding him to provide much needed nourishment; to calling on Romero, the orphanage handyman turned do-what-needs-to-be-done man to help with Juan's basic needs; to the act of fluffing his pillow; she did it all. These were the kind of giving, selfless acts that gave her more satisfaction than purchasing a painting for six figures ever had.

Shaking her head over her past and the things she used to consider important, she thanked God for showing her the true meaning of worth, love and service. That serving Him was all that mattered. She just wished she could get over the guilt that accompanied every thought of what her mother had done and the deaths she'd caused, including that of Amy's friend, Micah McKnight. Tears always accompanied thoughts of Micah. He'd been on a

SEAL mission in this very jungle, killed on the mission her mother had managed to gain information about. Her mother had then betrayed Micah.

Her mother. A woman so evil it scared her. She slapped the last of the medication into the cart with a thud, her breathing quickening with thoughts of the past. She would not turn out like her mother, she vowed on a daily basis. Amy would try her best to do everything in her power, with God's help, to make a difference in this world for the better. She'd started with revealing her mother's criminal activities, which resulted in saving Cassidy Mc-Knight's life; unfortunately, there was nothing she could do about Cassidy's brother, Micah. He was dead, his body never recovered. Now she was spending time helping here to make amends.

Amy swung away, hating the direction of her thoughts, yet unable to send them down a different path. Needing a distraction, she set out to find Juan to see if he needed anything. Her feet led her over to his curtained-off area. Absently she noted some retreating footfalls to her right. Pulling the curtain aside, she stopped and stared, shock and horror ripping through her. A pillow covered Juan's face, indentations from someone's grip fading as the foam slowly returned to its original shape. In the blink of an eye, she propelled herself to Juan's side and yanked the pillow from him.

"Lucas! Help!" she hollered even as she leaned over to check Juan's breathing. His lips had a blue tinge, his chest was still. Without a second thought, she pinched his nose, tilted his head back, placed her mouth over his and blew.

She came up for air, then leaned over him and blew again. And again.

More footfalls sounded behind her, this time running toward her, not away.

"What is it?" Lucas demanded.

On her next breath, without bothering to turn, she said, "He's not breathing."

Then she went down to force air into his lungs, once more pleading with God to make him breathe. Finally, with her next puff of life-giving air, Juan gasped, choked . . . and pulled in his own breath.

"Oh, thank You, Jesus." Amy slumped to the floor, shaking, trying to control her adrenaline rush and subsequent reactions while Lucas took over, checking Juan's vitals. He slipped an oxygen mask over Juan's face, cranking the knob to its highest level. Lucas patted his cheek. "Come on, man, open your eyes. Talk to me."

Juan's eyes flickered, opened and stared. He blinked. "What happened?" he mumbled around the mask.

Amy, still quivering, placed her fingers over her mouth, her gaze bouncing between Lucas and Juan to the pillow she'd tossed aside. "Someone tried to kill him," she whispered.

Lucas's eyes shot wide. He dropped the oxygen line and stared at her. "What?"

Juan's eyebrows dipped to the bridge of his nose as he processed her statement. She explained, "He must have been sleeping pretty deep. I came to check on him and found —" she gulped "— that pillow over his face. I pulled it off, hollering for you. He wasn't breathing so I started CPR."

"Did you see anyone?" Lucas asked. Juan watched them, not saying anything as he continued to suck in the oxygen — and the conversation. His color was better. Keeping her eyes on Juan but answering Lucas's question, she shook her head. "No, but I heard someone running away. If I hadn't come to check on him when I did . . ." She trailed off, unable to finish the thought.

"I'll give the chief of police a call and have him send someone out here to take a statement." He shrugged. "I wouldn't hold out hope for many results, though. David Ruibero's a good man, but there's only so much he can do with what he's got to work with."

Yeah, she knew how the justice system worked out here. Slower than Christmas two years away. "Well, we'll just have to keep a real close eye on him until he's able to take care of things himself." She glanced down at the man who'd fallen back asleep, his body traumatized by the recent event. She was sure he'd want details when he woke up.

Lucas went to make the call.

Two

Two weeks later, Amy still shuddered when she thought about coming upon Juan's lifeless form, the pillow cutting of his air. She felt sure she would carry that vision to her grave.

They'd informed the policeman who'd come to the orphanage to take a statement from Amy and Lucas about what they'd seen and heard. The officer had even packed up the pillowcase to see if his limited forensics department could find anything but didn't offer much encouragement, just as Lucas had warned.

Then Amy had filled Anna and Juan in on exactly what had happened. Juan had been puzzled, unable to comprehend why someone would want to kill him, but determined to find out once he gained his strength back.

Anna and Amy had taken turns keeping a vigilant eye on him until he'd grown strong enough to walk out of the gymnasium under his own power. Fortunately, nothing else had happened during that time.

Amy had also grown to care for Salvador Orozco and his little sister, Carlita, who, thankfully, had escaped the illness.

She'd gotten more of Salvador's story from Anna. Anna had explained Salvador was part of the kitchen staff and cleaning crew. When their family had been killed almost three years ago, he and his sister, Carlita, had lived on the streets before arriving on the doorstep of the orphanage about four months ago. Salvador had explained that he had trouble finding work that would allow him to bring Carlita along. There was no one he could leave her with, so they'd lived on what they could rummage, beg and steal. Only now he needed to leave her so he could find a way to provide for her. They couldn't live on the streets indefinitely.

Had the orphanage not provided him a job, he would have had to leave his only remaining family member behind. Anna had taken pity on the siblings, believing that being separated from Salvador would do Carlita further psychological damage. So, Salvador stayed and worked, cared for his sister and seemed to form a special attachment to Juan who had taken the young man under his wing.

When Juan asked about the siblings, concerned about their health, she told him, "Salvador and Carlita escaped the illness and everyone else is recovering nicely. Dr. Bennett did an outstanding job setting up the temporary hospital. Everyone has worked tirelessly, rotating just for sleeping and eating, so all the hard work and dedication is finally paying off, thank goodness. You're getting better."

Salvador's obvious anxiety about Juan's recuperation had him constantly at Juan's side. His continued insistence on exposing himself to illness exasperated her. "Salvador, you need to get out of here," she'd said.

"Is he going to die?"

"He'll be fine, it's just going to take a little while for his body to heal."

And Salvador would leave, only to return later in the day to ask, "Is he going to die?" Amy would assure him that Juan was not going to die. She finally left the young man alone. If he got sick, he got sick. He was already exposed, so it was really too late to worry about it now.

Now, almost everyone was on the road to recovery allowing her a little time to herself. She folded the last towel and placed it in the linen closet. Sharing a bathroom with three other relief workers wasn't exactly on her list of favorite things to do, but she was adjusting. For the first time in her life, she felt she was doing something that really mattered, something that was going to last longer than herself. She was making a difference.

Thank You, God. Keep using me, please. Thank You for allowing me to be here. You know how important it is for me to do this. I know I can never truly make right all the wrongs my mother's done, especially for the McKnight family. Because of her, Micah's dead. God, I feel so guilty, yet I know it's not my fault. I'm not the one who betrayed him, set him up to die, but it still hurts. So, thank You again for this opportunity to help. To make a difference, even if it is for just one person.

Immediately her thoughts went to Juan. She'd wondered what color his eyes were. When he'd opened them, she'd been stunned. His eyes were a blue-gray that seemed to see right into her very soul. They seemed so familiar, as if she should remember seeing those eyes somewhere before. Finally, she decided that it wasn't necessarily the color of his eyes, but the man behind them.

Stubborn as a mule, he continued to insist that he was strong enough to try to get up.

Each time she told him no. Each time, he insisted on trying. So, lips tight, she would sponge the sweat from his face and glare at him as he worked to get up. Although, lately, she had to admit that the last couple of times he'd gotten up, he'd actually stayed up awhile. Definitely an improvement.

A knock sounded on her door. "Come on in."

Anna stuck her head in. "Good morning."

Pulling her hair up into her functional ponytail, she mumbled around the rubber band she'd stuck in her mouth, "Morning. What brings you here so bright and early?"

"We had a new kid show up on our doorstep this morning."

Sadness shifted through her. She pulled the band from her mouth and wrapped it around the mass she held. "Oh. What happened this time?"

"I'm not sure." Anna planted herself on the bed. "He's not saying a whole lot. Just that his father died a couple of years ago and he has no other family. His name is Jonathas and he's seventeen years old. He's asking for a place to stay until he can find some work. I told him the rules, and he agreed to abide by them."

"Does he like construction? We could use some more workers to help with our new wing." Amy realized with a start she was using words such as *we* and *our* in conjunction with the orphanage. In such a short time, she already felt she belonged.

Anna's eye's brightened. "That's true. I'll ask him. Thanks for thinking of it."

"Not a problem."

Anna wiggled her eyebrows. "I have another reason for being here. *He* came looking for you."

"Who?" Amy asked, tongue in cheek. She knew exactly who *he* was.

"You know who."

"I'll be sure to find him shortly," she promised, turning away to hide the blush creeping up her neck. But still, tenderness filled Amy. Over the last few weeks, she'd come to care for the quiet, sometimes angry man — in spite of the fact that he drove her crazy with his stubborn independence.

"I told him you would be looking forward to having lunch with him."

"Anna!" Amy was fiery red at this point. She tossed the towel at her friend, smacking her in the face with it. Then the two women burst out laughing. It felt good. *Thank you, Lord, for laughter and friends in unexpected places.*

Juan gripped the twenty-pound weight in

his left arm, the weaker of the two, and hefted. Sweat dripped, his elbow dug into the thigh muscle right above his knee and he groaned. But he curled his arm up for a final count of twenty-five. He huffed, letting his arm drop. The weight clanked to the mat.

"Good job, there."

Juan looked up to see Lucas watching him with a concerned expression. "Hey," he grunted.

"You're pushing it a bit, aren't you?" Lucas asked.

Juan sucked in a deep breath. "Yep. Have to." In the weight room, off the now-empty gymnasium, he gave it his all, determined to regain his strength — again. The room had only been finished a week before the illness had started. The window stood open behind him, pulling out the smell of fresh wood and paint, replacing it with the muggy, humid air of the jungle. With his right hand, he massaged his quivering left bicep. "I can't let a little virus set me back on all the progress I've made."

"If you're not careful, you're going to pull or rupture something and undo all my hard work." Lucas's tone was dry, sarcastic.

Juan felt his laughter spurt in spite of himself. "*Your* hard work?"

31

Lucas strolled over to sit beside him on the bench. "Yeah, man. I didn't save your hide just to let you kill yourself, you know."

Juan felt the smile pulling the corner of his mouth. During the past year, the only thing that had kept him sane had been Lucas's dry sense of humor and sarcastic wit. He grabbed a scratchy towel and dried his face. "You know, I've never asked, and you've never said, but why did you fight so hard to save me? Anna told me how you sacrificed, gave up sleep, sometimes food, to spend hours trying to wake me up. Doing what needed to be done with my joints and muscles, to keep them from atrophying." Juan dropped the towel and looked his friend in the eye. "Why?"

Lucas shrugged, looked away. "Because."

"Because?"

"You were fighting too hard to live. How could I let you die?"

Juan had a feeling there was more to the story. "You know, Lucas, you're a real private person, and I respect that, but can't you give me a little more?"

Lucas sighed. "Chalk it up to a personal tragedy I didn't want to see happen again. My brother died in a fire — and I was too late to save him."

"Is that why you're so angry at God?"

"Partly."

"Do you believe in Him?"

Pursing his lips, Lucas nodded. "Yeah, I believe in Him."

That was all Juan was going to get from the man, he could tell. He changed the subject. "What do you think about the new nurse, Amy?"

Lucas cut his eyes to Juan, and Juan felt a flush start up his cheeks. To hide it, he leaned over to pick up the weight he'd just recently dropped. This time, he used his right hand.

"Why? You like her?"

Juan heard the smile in the doctor's question and couldn't help the snicker that escaped. "Do I *like* her?"

Lucas laughed. "I could set you up, you know."

"I don't want to be set up," Juan protested. "I just wondered what you thought about her."

"She's pretty," Lucas admitted.

"I can see that," Juan muttered, easily picturing her straight, perfectly cut blond hair and gorgeous blue eyes. The dimples in each cheek made his insides curl every time she flashed him a genuine smile. "I mean, what do think of her? Her personality? Her character? Would she be interested in someone who'll have . . . who can't . . ." He trailed off, embarrassed to express his thoughts even to his best friend.

Lucas became serious. "Someone who'll have scars the rest of his life and can't remember who he is?" Lucas finished the sentence for him.

"Yeah," he mumbled, focusing on curling the weight so he didn't have to look at Lucas.

"Well, I've only been around her for a few weeks, but I would say that she's the real deal. She's genuine, compassionate, great with kids . . . and she's hurting — maybe, healing. Sometimes her eyes are sad. But, she doesn't let it interfere with what she wants to get accomplished." Lucas punched him in the arm lightly. "I also think she's probably as stubborn as you are. She doesn't take no for an answer, or have you already noticed that?"

Juan snorted. "I've noticed."

"I figured you had. I'm also pretty sure she's a Christian."

"Why do you say that?" Juan looked up, startled. His friend never discussed religion. Avoided the topic as if it would contaminate him to even enter a discussion about God. Of course, Juan wasn't exactly sure what he, himself, thought about God and, not for the first time, wished he could remember. And yet he found himself praying more and more.

"She reads her Bible every morning out on the dock." The main orphanage building sat back away from one of the freshwater lakes scattered throughout the Amazon. Recently, a long dock had been added to allow swimming during the times it was safe and to provide easier river access. While Tefe was a small city with roads, water travel was still a necessity. Two new boats with outboard motors rocked gently, tied securely to the gleaming dock. Three canoes, the most common mode of travel, were banked on the shore.

Juan blinked. "She does?" He'd not known that. No wonder he couldn't find her this morning. Not that he'd been specifically looking for her. Okay, yes, he had. He'd just refused to acknowledge his disappointment when she hadn't come in to breakfast while he'd been there.

Whoosh.

Juan jumped as something flew past his cheek. "What . . . ?" He turned swiftly, and when he did, it threw him off balance. He landed on his rear.

Another soft, almost soundless, *whoosh* hissed by him.

"Get down!" Lucas yelled.

Juan wanted to say, I *am* down, but instead rolled to his right. *Thwap!* Something hit the mat beside him.

"What is it?" he hollered.

"Someone's shooting darts through the window," Lucas gasped as he grabbed Juan's arm. "Get your back against the wall. Don't be a target."

Juan panted, grunted, his muscles still quivering from his workout; his body still recovering from the virus. But he pushed himself against the wall and waited. He wanted to propel himself through the window and tackle the shooter. The urge was so strong, he shook with the effort to force himself still. But as he did, a flash of memory surfaced.

We've got a traitor. Get out, get out!

The explosion rocked him. Searing heat scorched the left side of his face. The child cried. They'd been betrayed, set up, sold out.

"Juan! Juan!"

Juan blinked, blinked again. Focused on Lucas. He was saying something, but Juan couldn't grasp the words. "What?"

"It's stopped. I'm going to try to find out who it was."

"I'm coming with you."

As they started for the door, Amy walked in.

"Amy!"

She jumped. "What? What's wrong?"

Juan gripped her forearms. "Did you see anyone outside the window? Running from the gym?"

"No. Why?"

"Someone was using us for target practice. Thank goodness for lousy aim." He looked at the two darts embedded in the wooden wall and the one in the mat on the floor.

Lucas said, "Come on, let's take a look around."

"I want to help. Which way should I go?" Amy asked.

Juan shook his head. "No way. This guy was trying to do some damage. I don't want you wandering around alone looking for him. In fact, why don't you head back to the main building and let Anna know what's going on. Call the police and have them send someone over. We'll look for our shooter."

Amy bit her lip, hesitated. "Okay." She turned and headed for the building.

Juan and Lucas split up, although Juan wondered what he'd do if he caught the guy. His overworked muscles told him he sure didn't have the strength for a fight.

Amy ran to the main building, told Anna what had happened, then decided to go back to the gym to see for herself what was going on. Entering the gymnasium through the side door, she made her way down the main hall to the weight room. She looked inside — and stopped abruptly. "Jonathas, what are you doing in here?"

The teen looked up, startled. "I was looking for Juan. He said he was going to work out some, then come over and help with the new wing. When he didn't show up, I came looking for him." He gestured to the wall. "What happened here?"

Amy looked at the three holes — two in the wall and one in the mat. The darts were gone. She said, "Someone tried to use darts to shoot Lucas and Juan." She blinked and asked Jonathas, "What happened to the darts? They were still there a few minutes ago."

Jonathas shrugged. "I don't know. I just got here and this is what I found when I walked in. Why would someone try to hurt either of them?"

"Good question," Juan answered from behind. Amy spun around and came nose to chest with the man. She stepped back, flustered. Juan frowned down at her and said, "I thought you were going back to the main building."

Why did she feel guilty? "I did, but then I decided to come here and just . . . see . . . whatever. I don't know what I expected to find. Something."

"Where are the darts?" Lucas asked, frowning.

Amy shrugged. "I have no idea. They were gone when I got here. Jonathas came looking for you and said they were gone when he got here, too."

Lucas growled. "Should have collected and bagged those before going on our wild-goose chase. The guy probably watched us leave, then rounded the corner, came in here and pulled his evidence." He raked a hand through his sandy blond hair. Dark eyes glittered with frustration under his brows.

Juan stomped over to the wall, studying the hole. "You think anything was on the tips of those darts?"

Lucas looked startled. "What? Like poison?"

"Yeah."

Amy swallowed hard. Poison? And why did Juan all of a sudden look extremely familiar? Seeing just the right side of his face, in profile, without the scars, he reminded her of someone. The way he tilted his head, the quirk of his lips. She racked her brain but couldn't pull a name from it.

Juan looked at Lucas. "You got a pocket-knife on you?"

Lucas handed it over. "What are you doing?"

"Well, if there was poison on the tips of those things, some of the residue would be left in this wood." He flicked the knife open. "Now, I just need a plastic Baggie."

Amy bit back surprised laughter. Plastic Baggie? He'd sounded so . . . professional up to that point. She moved to the first-aid kit that hung on the wall.

"Here," she said pulling out the Brazilian version of the Ziploc bag. "Your plastic Baggie."

Juan smiled his thanks and his eyes glinted. He'd seen her humor and appreciated it.

With the knife, he scraped around the hole left by the dart and caught the shavings in the plastic bag. "Could I have two more?"

Amy shook off her thoughts; told herself it wasn't important and complied. "What do you need two more for?"

Juan explained as he worked. "Well, there

were three different darts. I want samples from the three different holes. I'm just curious. If there was something like poison on the tips, was it all the same or was there something different on each one — or something on one, but not the others?" He exchanged the second bag for the third. This time, he used the knife to cut a patch around the hole in the mat and then placed the entire specimen in the bag.

Once all three were filled, sealed and labeled, he looked at Lucas. "Will the police department be able to do a better job with this than they have with finding out who I am or who tried to kill me once before?"

He sounded bitter, and Amy's heart ached for him. Lucas shrugged. "I don't know. Leave me some of the shavings and I'll look at them under a microscope. We'll give the rest to the police and hope for the best. If they don't come up with anything, I can have everything shipped to the States for examination. I have some friends on the police force in South Carolina."

Amy got two more bags, and the men worked on preserving some of the samples. Jonathas watched the proceedings in silence. Finally, everything that could be done was done. Amy looked at Juan and asked, "How do you know so much about evidence collection? What are you? A forensics guy or something?"

THREE

How do you know so much about evidence collection?

The question tormented him. How did he know what to do? The work felt natural, second nature, as if he'd done it before. He closed his eyes and searched his brain. Then he groaned with frustration. *Why* couldn't he remember?

He'd had CAT scans, MRIs, everything. Lucas had donated both of the extremely expensive machines to the hospital — and used them on Juan. Nothing showed up as permanent damage. In fact, his last scan showed his brain had fully recovered from his head trauma.

And yet — he couldn't remember.

God, are you there? I honestly believe I can say I believe in You. So, can you help me? Please?

He opened his eyes and looked at Amy, who stood waiting for an answer to her question. He wished he had one to give. He shrugged. "I don't know."

Amy's eyes conveyed sympathy and she turned to Jonathas. "Well, guess that's it for the excitement around here. Anyone ready for something to eat?"

Jonathas flashed a rare smile. "Always." He headed toward the cafeteria located off the side of the main building.

Amy saw Salvador and Carlita walking with several other children. She waved and smiled. Salvador waved back; Carlita stuck a finger in her mouth, but at least she didn't turn away this time. In fact, she even offered Amy a shy smile. Progress.

Lucas said, "I'll call the police and talk to the chief, see if he wants to come out here. My guess is he'll just tell me to bring him the evidence. There's a small lab here in Tefe. Any big stuff has to be sent to Manaus or São Paulo."

He headed off, and Juan turned to Amy. "Walk with me along the river? I'm not very hungry right now. My appetite is still trying to work its way back to normal."

She smiled. "Sure."

They headed down the path that led to the river and he asked, "What are you doing here, Amy?"

Juan watched her hesitate, her delicate

brows drawing together into a frown. "What do you mean?"

He wanted to ask her all about herself, her background, find out what made her tick. The sadness he sometimes saw flicker in her eyes told him she had a depth to her that he was interested in trying to discover. What had happened in her life to shadow her beautiful eyes? "Just, why here? Why this orphanage? You're very passionate about helping. More so than the average person." He shrugged. "I guess I'm just curious as to why."

She kept walking, turning her head as she thought. He wished she hadn't, he wanted to see her face. Finally, she said, "Because of my mother."

"Your mother?"

"Mmm, hmm. Because of her, I want to spread goodness, kindness, compassion, everything good you can think of. I want to be a part of it, helping others, telling them about Christ."

Was she for real? "That's — admirable."

Amy ducked her head self-consciously. "Well, I don't know about that. It's just how I feel right now. The decision I've made. And I hope God honors it."

"God, huh?"

She nodded, looked up at him. "Yes, God. Why?"

Juan stuck his hands into his pockets and scuffed the mud path. "I wish I knew what I thought about Him. I mean, I listen to the speaker in the little chapel every Sunday, but . . ."

"Yes, I like him. We're fortunate he's willing to come out here each week. And he's definitely on target when he talks about the Bible. But what do you think? About God?"

"I'm not sure. I mean, I believe there *is* a God. But at this point, I can't remember if I ever . . ." He felt weird having this conversation, but good at the same time. She listened in a way that made him want to keep talking. "You know. Asked him for forgiveness. Did the whole salvation thing. Sometimes I talk to Him like He's my best friend. Other times I wonder if I'm talking to air. Do you think He holds that against me?"

"I know what you mean. And, of course He doesn't hold that against you. I finally came to not only understand, but accept, that He loves me, regardless of the things I've done. In spite of my family, and just simply because He created me, He loves me. I used to wonder if He was up there in His great big Heaven, looking down on me, ready to catch me doing something wrong so He could zap me." A dimple peeked up at him as she gave a cheeky grin. "Thank goodness that's not the case. I'd have been zapped a long time ago." The grin faded, her eyes turned sad. "He just wants to love me — and just wants me to believe that, which I do, even though I don't understand unconditional love. I just know I'm grateful for it." She gave a sad little laugh that matched the look in her eyes, and Juan felt it seep into the cracks of his hurting soul.

Amy moved, stepping over the trunk of a small tree to use it as a seat. Juan settled himself beside her and looked up to see the sun sprinkling light between the huge canopy leaves above him. The forest was alive, never still, always moving. He'd come to love it . . . and hate it, for it was here that he'd lost himself. And sometimes it was extremely hard to hold on to the hope that he would one day remember.

Changing the subject, he asked, "So what do you think about the place? The kids, the staff?"

She took the hint. "I love it here. I can't believe all the good going on here in what seems to be the middle of nowhere. I have peace knowing I made the right decision in coming. I wasn't sure at first, but when

Anna called to ask for my help —" she shrugged "— I couldn't say no."

He gazed off into the distance and murmured, "Well, I'm sure glad you're here. I just wish I knew how *I* got here, what I was doing before the fire, who I've left . . ." He glanced back down at her. "I don't know what I would've done without you while I was so sick." He swallowed hard; her beauty moved him. Not just the outward, but what she was on the inside. Compassionate, caring . . . all the things Lucas had mentioned. "Thank-you seems kind of inadequate after all you did for me, not just medically, but emotionally, too. Your being there helped tremendously." Juan gave a small self-deprecating laugh. "It's hard to admit, but I really felt alone. I've felt that way for a long time. I mean, Lucas has been great, but . . ." He shrugged, unable to fully find the words to share his thoughts.

Amy reached over and placed a compassionate hand on his forearm. "Keep talking to God. He's there and He hears you. Come join me in the morning at the end of the dock. I go there to be alone with God, but wouldn't mind your company." She smiled. "And in the meantime, you're doing some great stuff around here. I hear you got Salvador playing baseball and laughing.

That's an accomplishment. You've obviously made a huge impact on him. He came to your bedside just about every day to watch over you. He kept asking me if you were going to die." She glanced up at him with a shy smile. "I'm very glad you didn't."

He gave in to the desire to wrap an arm around her shoulders for a quick squeeze. "Thanks."

Letting his arm drop, he changed the topic. "I wish we could do something to help Carlita. She needs a special kind of help that's not readily available here."

They stood, brushed themselves off and started walking along the river's edge, through the path worn from many trips for water. Amy mused, "In the States, there's a child psychologist on every corner. But here . . ."

"We could offer to fly her to America for help."

Amy shrugged. "True, but . . ."

The trees rustled more so than usual, distracting her from finishing her sentence. Juan stopped. He wasn't terribly worried, but a stray jaguar had been known to attack the unwary tourist who wandered into its territory. And sometimes two-legged beasts often roamed looking for prey. It paid to be cautious. He scanned the area, senses on alert, wary, watchful.

"What is it?" Amy whispered, catching his suddenly intense mood.

"I don't think it's anything, but let's get back to the orphanage. I'm starting to get hungry." He wasn't about to scare her with the jaguar theory — or take a chance that it was something even more dangerous. Better just to get away now. He took her hand and turned around to head back when a memory flashed.

"Catch the ball, dude." He passed the basketball to the guy on his right and watched the man shoot a perfect, net-only basket. He whooped and thumped the guy on the back. "Now, that's what I call shooting!"

Another flash.

The jungle, betrayal, fire. "Get out now!" The words ripped through his headphone. He looked back at the frightened eyes of the small child. "Come on, little one, we've got to go." He gripped the small hand tight and pulled. The explosion rocked him, he lost his grip. "No!"

Another flash.

"Gabe, look out!" He pulled the trigger. The man stopped in shock, looked at the stain spreading across his chest, then staggered, fell forward and was still. Hard to breathe.

Singed flesh stung his nose. Then . . . nothing.

Juan stumbled on with each clip of memory. He'd make sure Amy was safe, then examine what he'd just remembered. Excitement rippled through him. He was remembering. *Oh, God, please let me remember.*

Amy let Juan lead her back down the path; he hurried and she stumbled along behind him. The river rushed beside them. Juan kept looking over his shoulder.

"You think someone's there?" she gasped between steps. "Why would someone be watching us?"

Juan glanced back again, "I'm not sure anyone is. But those darts didn't come from nowhere, so I'm just going to be a little paranoid until we can figure that out."

Amy, seeing his point, kept up the pace. Juan turned back one more time to look at her and before Amy could warn him, he ran into a low-hanging branch. It snagged his shirt and held on. Juan grunted, jerked away. The shirt ripped leaving a gaping hole and Amy gasped; her hands flying up to cover her mouth.

"I'm all right," he reassured her. "It didn't

get much of me, just ruined a perfectly good shirt."

Amy stared at the gap left by the torn garment. She couldn't take her eyes from the exposed skin.

Juan saw her staring and flushed. "I know. It's not pretty, is it?"

His puckered, tortured skin looked angry, shouting its fury at the devastation the fire had left behind. Amy realized he thought she was horrified by the scars, and she was, but that was only secondary in her mind. It was the birthmark over the lower part of his abdomen twining its way around to his back that had her transfixed.

"Oh, I'm so sorry," she whispered through her fingers. She dropped her hands from her mouth to reach out as though to touch him, pulling back at the last second. Shock still shuddered through her. She couldn't think, couldn't breathe.

He glanced around behind her, then reached out and cupped her chin with his good hand, free of scars or ugly reminders. "Hey, it's all right. Every time I see them, I just tell myself it's better than the alternative." Again he looked around, studied the bushes, the trees, but nothing moved. And still, Amy stared at him.

Tears leaked down her cheeks to mingle

with the sweat already there. He shifted and through her fog, she sensed he'd become uncomfortable with her stare. "Do they repulse you?"

Amy jerked. "No, no, of course not. I've actually seen worse."

"Then, come on. Let's get on back. I don't think anyone is there, but . . ." He took her hand again and tugged.

Amy followed mindlessly, still in a state of utter disbelief, danger forgotten. How many times had she seen that birthmark as she swam in the pool at the McKnight estate? It looked like a belt, complete with the buckle right above his navel. Only it stopped short under his ribs on the left side of his torso. How often had she teased him about having to get a tattoo so that he could finish what nature had started? She remembered how he'd laughed when she'd bought him a pair of suspenders to go with his "belt" the Christmas she'd been seventeen and he'd been home on leave from the Navy.

Hysteria bubbled to the surface. Emotions ran rampant, her heart thudded in her ears. She had to find a phone, get in contact with his family. She had to tell them their prayers had been answered, that she'd found their missing son and brother. She'd found Micah McKnight.

■ ■ ■ ■

Three days later, Amy finished up her lunch and tossed her napkin on the tray. Exhaustion swamped her and sleep eluded her. She'd called every number she had for every member of the McKnight family several times over, including her best friend, Cassidy, Micah's sister. No answer. They were all on an extended cruise, apparently out of cell phone range.

And there was no way she was leaving that kind of information on voice mail. So, while she'd absorbed and processed the fact that Micah McKnight was alive and well — at least for the most part — she still wrestled with what to do now. Did she tell him she knew who he was? And that her mother had been the one to betray him, the one who'd caused all of his misery?

That Amy's eagerness to help at the orphanage had been influenced, in part, by her devastation when she'd learned of her mother's illegal activities? Activities which included murder, human trafficking and the kidnapping of Amy's best friend, Cassidy McKnight, who had travelled to this very orphanage to take custody of a child left in her care.

Did she tell him her mother had been so blinded by greed, so desperate to find a way to stop Cassidy's father, the ambassador to Brazil, from continuing his work against human trafficking that she'd planned Cassidy's kidnapping, then hired her own brother, Amy's uncle Rafael, to finish the job after Cassidy escaped the kidnappers?

She shuddered at that thought. Oh no, no way was she taking on that responsibility. Uh-uh. *You wouldn't ask me to do that, would You, God? Please don't ask me to do that.*

Amy choked back a sob and decided she needed a distraction. Not only had she been thinking about Micah nonstop ever since their dash through the jungle, she'd been thinking about the fact that she had family somewhere in this country. Could she find them? And if she were to go on a search for relatives, where did she start?

Thinking it through, she decided she could start with the names she had. As far as where, she knew that her mother's picture had been on the wall of the police station as recently as two years ago. It could still be there. If so, she could ask questions. Juanita Morales, Amy's mother, had been born in the slums of Brazil and sold into prostitution by her older brother. She'd finally managed to escape to the United States, where she'd studied how the rich lived and learned well. She'd changed her name, married a senator and life was good.

Unfortunately, it had been when she'd found out her husband was broke that she'd turned to a life of crime, a life she was intimately familiar with — human trafficking. Only a few months ago, Amy had learned the truth of her mother's background after she'd discovered incriminating information on her mother's computer, implicating her in Micah McKnight's disappearance. Through a fluke, while on a mission here in Tefe, Brazil, Micah had discovered the woman's true identity and e-mailed a copy of the wanted poster to Amy's father. Before the man had a chance to open the e-mail, her mother had confiscated it and set her evil plan in motion. She'd set Micah up to die, betraying two teams of SEALs, one of them Micah's team.

Amy shuddered at the memories. *Oh, Lord, help me. I have to tell him I know him. But first I need to talk to Lucas. I need to make sure it's okay medically to tell him. So until Lucas comes back to the orphanage, help me get in touch with his family members — and continue to help me find mine.*

Thinking about what she had to go on, Amy considered her options. She had two names — well, three, really, if she counted her mother. Rafael Morales, her uncle, Juanita Morales, her mother, and a woman named Maria. The latter was the woman who'd looked after Cassidy while Cassidy had been held hostage in the camp. Cassidy said that the woman had faced down Rafael, so obviously she had some kind of power, Amy just wasn't sure what kind or why.

Amy decided her best course of action would be to start with the local police. She notified Anna that she had some errands to run, and Anna had offered her the jeep and given her a list of supplies to pick up while she was in town. Thirty teeth-rattling minutes later, she parked in front of the police station. She'd not bothered to ask for directions since the town was small, and she figured she could find the building on her own.

Sure enough, a short tour up and down the streets had familiarized her with the layout of the town, and she'd had no trouble locating the police station. Although the town was small, it had a good number of officers on the force to fight the drug-smuggling trade that was popular along the one thousand miles of coastland where Tefe and other cities connected to the Amazon.

57

Amy climbed out of the jeep and slammed the door. She walked up the three wooden steps that led to the front door of the police station and pushed her way inside. Standing in the entrance, she scanned the place, taking in the details. She could see several metal desks, telephones, an open door leading to the cells in the back. Then she spotted the Missing posters on the wall next to the Wanted Persons. And there was her mother — thirty years ago, listed as a missing person. Amy felt her heart clench, nausea swirled and she fought it down. The black-and-white picture was grainy and faded, but Amy had no doubt who the young girl was. Sold into prostitution at the age of fifteen. By Amy's uncle, Raphael Morales. Anger bubbled unexpectedly inside Amy.

"What a legacy you two left," she spat.

"Excuse me?" a voice asked in heavily accented English.

Amy whirled around and found herself staring at a uniform. She let her eyes travel up . . . and up. The man before her stood at least six feet five inches tall. Stepping back, she swallowed hard and somehow managed a smile.

She held out a hand. "Hello, I'm Amy Graham. I'm new to Tefe and just thought I would familiarize myself with the city."

Black eyes narrowed, suspicion glinted, but he held out his hand and engulfed hers. In a lilting Portuguese accent, he asked, "What may I do to help you, Ms. Graham?"

Taking her hand back, Amy cleared her throat, "Please, call me Amy. I . . . was just looking over your posters."

"I am David Ruibero, the chief of police for the town of Tefe. Now what kind of interest would you have in my posters?" Not a lot of people outside of the orphanage spoke English. Or Spanish. Portuguese was definitely the language to know around here. She'd had Cassidy tutor her before leaving the States and she'd listened to her language CDs on the plane, but if she had to carry on a full-fledged adult conversation, she'd be in trouble.

"That one," she blurted. Cassidy had described Maria to perfection. The woman was wanted for harboring fugitives, rebels, murderers, slave traffickers. Amy looked for a name at the bottom of the poster, but it had faded and she couldn't make it out. The picture, though, was pretty clear. Maria's thick, brown face looked black in the picture; her eyes were cold stones in a face that looked as if it had been made to be wreathed in dimpled smiles. But no smiles showed here. Her lips stretched tight and flat across her face and her nose looked as if it had been broken once. But she'd protected Cassidy from her kidnappers. That told Amy that there was the possibility of goodness somewhere under all that hardness and hate. She hoped. "Who is she?"

Suspicion remained in the dark eyes, and he hesitated before answering, "Maria Morales. Why?"

Amy gasped, and the room spun. "Morales?" she squeaked.

"Here, sit down. Now, why does that name shock you?"

She slumped into the offered seat and buried her face in her hands. Would the nightmare never end? Would every member of her family that she found turn out to be evil?

David Ruibero had the appearance of a gentle giant, yet Amy wouldn't want to cross him in a back alley. She had a feeling his softness was all a cover, that he could strike as quick as a snake. Intelligence gleamed in his black eyes. No way was she telling this man that the woman on the wall was her maternal grandmother. "Um, no reason. I think my blood sugar's a bit low." She brushed aside his interest in her shock and asked, "Do you know where she is? Have you found her?"

David Ruibero sat back and studied her. "You have your reasons for asking?"

Amy sighed. The man was too shrewd, and she knew her face was an open book. "Yes, I have my reasons. Do you mind if I don't share them at the moment? I'm still trying to figure out . . ." she trailed off.

He clasped his hands in front of him. "All right. No. We haven't found her. Don't really expect to, to be honest. She's part of a rebel group that is so deep in the jungle, so well armed and protected that even if we knew her exact location, we'd probably lose too many lives trying to infiltrate. An undercover operation would be the way to go, but we don't have anyone with the skills to do that on the force . . . right now, anyway. If we had help from some of your Rangers or SEALs —" he shrugged "— or if one of the rebels could be bought off, that might work, but they are all extremely loyal to their cause — and each other."

"How do I get the word out that I'm looking for her?"

For the first time since she'd met him, his eyes reflected something other than suspicion. This time, surprise mixed with wariness flashed at her. "You don't want to do that. That, my dear American, would be very hazardous to your health."

"Not to mention stupid."

Amy swiveled her head to see another uniformed officer enter the room.

David said, "Ah, Roberto, how nice of you to join us. May I introduce one of the relief workers from the Amazon orphanage? This is Ms. Amy Graham. She is busy making herself familiar with our little town."

"Busy setting herself up for trouble, if you ask me. Don't stick your nose where it doesn't belong, lady."

Amy flinched at the hostility in his heavily accented tone. What was *his* problem? Probably in his midforties, he was a short, round little man with a bald head and beady black eyes. A salt-and-pepper mustache sat neatly upon his upper lip. He spoke excellent English, too. Most natives didn't understand American idioms. The one he'd used had rolled smoothly from his tongue.

"Trouble?" Amy arched a brow, refusing to let his attitude intimidate her.

"Yes. Why do you want to go looking for that one?"

Amy swallowed hard. How much did she dare reveal? "I . . . might have some information about a family member of hers."

Roberto laughed. "Family? And how would you know about any family she might have? Her family is either dead or soon will be."

Amy shivered and stood. He gave her the creeps, and the chief wasn't jumping in to help, although the look he gave Roberto told her the man didn't normally talk like this in the chief's presence. She stood, looking back and forth between the men. "Listen, if you know how to contact her, I want to talk to her. Otherwise, never mind." She focused on David. "Thank you for the information. I appreciate the help." What little it had been.

Amy stepped toward the door, and Roberto slid in front of her, blocking her exit. Nervousness clenched her midsection, but she met his eyes and raised her chin, keeping silent, waiting on him.

Finally, he stepped aside. "Watch your back, *senhorita.* This is not a good place to make enemies. Not if you want to live very long."

Amy sucked in a breath, acknowledged his warning — or threat — with a nod, waved goodbye to David and hurried out the door.

FOUR

Where was she? Juan wondered. He'd planned to ask Amy to eat with him, but she was nowhere to be found. So he'd found a table with Jonathas and Salvador, yet couldn't help wondering what Amy was doing.

When she didn't return in time for lunch, he finished up and decided to lie down for a while. He hated to admit that he needed to rest, but his body had flashed neon warnings in the form of a throbbing headache and aching muscles. When he woke up two hours later, his headache was gone and Amy still hadn't returned. He questioned Anna, who said she'd gone into town to run a few errands. He stayed busy on the wing, waiting for her to get back.

Lucas declared it was good therapy for building his stamina back up. Now, as he worked, his eyes kept straying to the plastic-covered opening, hoping to catch a glimpse of the dark blond head or slender profile. Juan shook his head. He couldn't allow himself to fall for her. He had no idea who he was. He didn't even have a real name.

Shrugging those thoughts off, he watched Salvador and Jonathas work together, building the opposite wall. The two had hit it off pretty well despite their age difference. The wall was coming together and the wing should be finished before too long.

He slammed the hammer onto the nail. *Bam.*

And the memory was there. He jerked, sat with a thump on the wooden floor. *The jungle smell — wet, fresh, teeming with life. He hefted the machete and chopped another vine out of his path. Men followed. The mansion sat just ahead. The other SEALs were in the water. His job was to disarm the alarm system. Someone else listened in on everything as he monitored the mission.*

"You almost done with that part of the wall?"

Juan whirled to find Romero, the orphanage's resident handyman, standing behind him. A large dark man in a sweat-drenched white tank top, the tattoo on his left upper bicep rippled on top of bulging muscles. His tool belt hung low on his lean hips, and his white teeth flashed in the blazing sun, competing with the gleam of matching gold in his nose and ear.

The memory still spun through Juan's mind like a movie out of control. He cleared his throat and said, "Uh, yeah. Just taking a little break." He wiped the sweat from his brow with the towel he kept stuffed in the back pocket of his green cargo shorts.

Why was he tramping through the jungle with a team of SEALs? Where was the mansion that he could now picture in detail? Had he been a SEAL?

"Miss Anna sent this out to you." Romero handed Juan a plastic cup full of ice-cold lemonade. He downed it in one swallow, his mind still rippling from the memory. *Obrigado.*

"Welcome."

Thunder rumbled, and Romero looked at the sky. "Storm's coming."

Juan peered up through a break in the canopy above him and eyed the restless sky that only moment ago had been cloudy but sunny. Now the clouds rolled and swirled, obliterating the sun. Thunder boomed and a flash of lightning encouraged him to hurry and put away his tools.

He called to the teens who were packing up, "Come on guys, we're done here. Let's get inside before we get soaked — or electrocuted."

The young men wasted no time gathering their things, and the four of them headed for the plastic door that led to the newly renovated main building. Salvador walked beside him down the brightly lit hallway. "How're you doing, Sal?"

Salvador's shoulders lifted in a shrug. "All right, I guess."

"How's Carlita? Has she spoken yet?"

Salvador took a deep breath. "She will be fine. She will speak when she is ready. Everyone just needs to stop trying to force her. She is my family. *I* will take care of her."

The intensity of the young man's words hit Juan. He studied Salvador and saw the fierce love for his sister reflected there. "Maybe you're right, Sal. We just want to see her get better, that's all."

Salvador swallowed hard, visibly forcing himself to relax. "I know, Senhor Juan, I just want to help her and don't know how, sometimes it makes me . . ." He broke off and gave a sheepish smile. "Sorry."

Juan's heart ached for this brother of the young girl. So much responsibility at such a young age. He should be getting ready to graduate college, be enjoying his youth, discovering his place in the world. Instead, his family was dead and he had a little girl to raise. "I know. You're doing a great job. Still, I wish she could see a child psychologist or some kind of counselor."

Salvador threw his shoulders back and said, "Thank you for your concern, *senhor.* I think I will go see if she is ready to go to supper."

Juan watched the young man branch off to the right to head down to the room he shared with his sister. That was one thing Juan really liked about this orphanage. They didn't separate siblings. They kept them together as much as possible. Salvador and Carlita shared a suite with another brother and sister pair. It was a dorm-room design. Twin beds sat on opposite walls, with a bathroom in between the two rooms. There was a short wall that allowed privacy when changing clothes in the room. Each child had a chest of drawers and shared a small closet for hanging clothes. Some of the older teens even had televisions in their rooms that got certain approved channels from the satellite dish. Of course, if one wished to have living quarters separate from his or her sibling that could be arranged, too. Most orphanages had a boys' living area and a girls' living area.

Juan stepped inside the temporary tool storage room and set his tool belt on the shelf. The construction crew from Manaus had been hired to do most of the work with funds from donations, but Anna was very careful with the expenditures. By allowing some of the orphanage workers to help, it provided jobs for those who otherwise wouldn't be working. And besides, construction out here in the jungle moved slowly. The intermittent storms often sent the main workers home early. But those laborers from the orphanage could wait out the storm and then go back to work.

Juan headed to his private staff room to shower and get ready for supper himself.

"*Senhor?*"

Juan stopped and turned. Jonathas approached him and asked, "*Senhor,* did you find out about the darts from the gym?"

Juan studied the young man. "No, we haven't heard anything yet. Why?"

Jonathas shrugged. "I was just wondering."

Was he really just wondering or was there more to it than that? After all, the darts were gone when he and Lucas arrived on the scene — and Jonathas was there. But he had a legitimate reason for being there. Juan himself had told the boy to come find him when he was ready to work on the orphanage wing. And yet . . .

Juan clapped Jonathas on the back and said, "I'll let you know when I hear something."

"Okay. See you at supper." The boy turned back. "Oh, hey, don't forget the picnic tomorrow."

"What picnic?"

"The one I hear they have every year. They even have a dunking booth. Get ready to get soaked." He disappeared around the corner.

Juan grumbled, "Oh, yeah, that picnic. Who says I'm gonna volunteer?"

The next morning, right before sunrise, Amy continued her daily tradition of her dockside quiet time. Her stomach was still in knots, and she needed some guidance. After calling the McKnight family again — and again getting no answer, she gathered her Bible and notebook and headed out, only to come across Jonathas in the jeep driving toward her. She called, "Good morning. You're up early."

The seventeen-year-old pulled up to a stop next to her and said, "*Bom dia, senhorita*. My morning routine. I am driving down to check on the cows." The cattle meant a lot to the orphanage as they provided milk and meat. Often they were sold to raise money for other necessities that the orphanage needed in order to keep running efficiently.

Amy smiled. "You're doing a great job, Jonathas."

Bright white teeth flashed in the morning light. "Thank you." He disappeared in a trail of dust, and Amy continued on to the dock. Walking to the end of the fifty-foot pier, she sat and looked out over the muddy brown water, catching glimpses of the wildlife that never ceased to amaze her. A caiman floated past. Then another. And another. Nocturnal creatures, it was still early enough for them to be out and about. They looked like alligators, their snouts skimming the top of the water.

The first time she'd had her quiet time out here, she'd had her legs hanging over the edge of the dock. Then she'd seen her early-morning companions and nearly had a coronary. Today, she didn't even flinch. This was her favorite time of the day. The sun rose with a blend of orange, yellows and reds, first peeking above the horizon, then coming forth in its full glory to proudly display God's handiwork. It never failed to take her breath away.

When the sun finished its climb, she pulled out her Bible and just sat without

71

opening it. Instead, she went straight to the point. *What do I do, Lord? What do I say? Should I talk to Lucas and ask him what to do? Would it do more damage to Micah — er, Juan — no, Micah, if I bring up the past and . . .* She groaned and dropped her head in her hands.

"Problems?"

She jumped. It was Micah's voice — but it wasn't. It was deeper, with a rasp he didn't used to have. Due to the damage from smoke inhalation, no doubt.

Amy turned and looked up at him, seeing the resemblance all over again. She'd noticed it in the beginning, but had never entertained the possibility that he might actually be Micah. Because Micah was dead. Only now he stood looking at her with a frown creasing his forehead.

She frowned back. "Problems? A few. God and I were just having a conversation about them. Well, actually, I was talking and He was listening." Then she smiled. "What are you doing here so early?"

Micah sighed and dropped his head. "Looking for you. I was wondering if I could join you."

"Sure." Amy could see he had something on his mind. "What's up?" She did her best to sound cheery and carefree. No need to let him see her turmoil until she could talk to Lucas and get in touch with his family. Surely one of them would see she'd tried to call and call her back. She'd gotten a satellite phone, and both Cassidy and the ambassador had the number. Hopefully, he'd check in with his office and they'd give him the message that she wanted to talk to him.

Micah sat down beside her, crossed his legs and rested his elbows on his knees with his hands clasped loosely in front of him. Silent, he stared down in the muddy water.

Amy waited and inhaled his freshly showered scent. He looked good this morning, muscles gleaming in the morning sun. He had on short sleeves and didn't seem to mind the scars prominently displayed on his left arm. Silent, she remained patient, allowing him to find the words he seemed to be searching for.

Finally, he blew out a breath and said, "I'm sorry if my scars offended you."

Was *that* what he thought?

"Oh, no," she reached out impulsively and laid a hand on his scarred left hand. "Why would you think that?"

He looked her in the eye, "Because of the way you reacted in the woods after the dart incident. You were . . . repulsed. And I've noticed you've been avoiding me these last few days."

Amy caught her breath and stemmed the tears that threatened to fall. Although she had been avoiding him, it wasn't because of his scars. She protested, "I wasn't offended or repulsed, I . . . hurt for you. I can't believe what you've been through. You . . . you're . . . I wish . . ." She stopped, sucked in air and said, "I can't even explain the feelings that went through me yesterday. I wish I could, but, please believe me, your scars don't bother me. No, they're not pretty, but they represent your strength, your courage. The fact that you can even walk shows what a fighter you are."

A thought occurred to her, and she grabbed her Bible, flipping the pages, "Here, I want to read you something. It's in I Samuel 16:7. The last part of the verse says, 'The Lord does not look at the things man looks at. Man looks at the outward appearance, but the Lord looks at the heart.' "

Micah reached out and ran a finger down the page in her Bible. Softly, he asked, "And you think He's looking at my heart?"

Amy nodded. "I know He is . . . and I promise, I am, too."

Light flared in his eyes, hope, tenderness . . . fear. Micah stared back out over the water, clearing his throat. "Thank you.

Amy, I know we haven't known each other that long, and I'm not sure what the future holds for me, but . . ." He caught her eye, and Amy sucked in a breath at the look. No, no, she couldn't let him say anything. Not yet. Not until she told him everything.

"Here," she blurted, "this will help. Start with John." She handed her Bible over to him. He took it reluctantly, obviously wanting to finish what he'd started to say. She stood. "I'll just leave you and God to have a talk."

He hefted the Bible and smiled up at her. "You don't have to leave."

"I need to go in and help get the little ones ready for breakfast anyway. You can give me the Bible later."

"All right. I think maybe I will just sit here for a while — see what God has to say."

Amy walked up the dock and turned up the path, passing the gymnasium. She looked back to see Micah sitting with the Bible in his lap. At least it was open. She whispered a prayer. "Reveal Yourself to him, Lord. Show him Your love and goodness."

Only a few steps later, she heard a rumble in the distance and saw the jeep heading back her way, occasionally catching a glimpse of it between the trees. Jonathas must have finished with the cows early. She picked up her pace, stopped and looked back. The trees were in the way, but it looked as if the jeep had stopped on the dock. The front faced the end where Micah still sat. How strange. It just sat there, idling . . . no, wait, it was moving. Why would someone drive the jeep on the dock? She moved to get a better look.

Then the vehicle was rolling on the downward sloping dock, down toward the end where Micah sat. Picking up speed quickly, soon it would be right on him!

"Juan!" she screamed.

Surely, Micah would feel the vibration of the dock and look up, hear it as it got closer. Who was driving? A quick glance showed an empty driver's seat. Horror swept over her. Sure enough, the jeep was bearing down on Micah and he had nowhere to go except into the river where the caimans still swam.

FIVE

Amy screamed his name again as she raced back toward the dock. She saw him turn around and frown as he caught sight of the jeep heading toward him. He waited, puzzlement creasing his forehead. He was thinking the vehicle would stop, but he didn't know what Amy did — no one was driving. Realization dawned for him almost too late as she watched him make the split-second decision to roll into the water. The jeep slammed into the river a few seconds later, grille first.

"Juan!"

Where was he? Had the jeep landed on top of him when it hit the water? She climbed down the bank and waded into the shallow part of the river, desperately searching for him.

Scanning the surface of the murky river, she still didn't see any sign. *Oh, God, please let him be okay. Help me find him.* She went under and opened her eyes, but visibility was nil. Terror choked her as she pushed aside thoughts of caimans, piranhas and other dangers while reaching, feeling for Micah. Nothing. She searched until her burning lungs forced her back to the surface.

Breaking through, she spat, gasped and breathed in air. Something grabbed her ankle and she screamed, choked on more water and kicked at the vise around her lower leg. But it held on. Then she was free as Micah surged before her. Her pounding heart eased as she realized he was the one who'd grabbed her foot. He'd latched on to her to help him find his way up.

"Are you okay?" he demanded. "Are you crazy coming into the river like this?"

She gasped, "I had to find you."

"I'm fine. Swim for the shore." He looked around and froze. Amy looked in the direction he stared and choked back another scream as one of the caimans she'd watched earlier headed their way. Fast. "Oh, Lord, help."

"Swim, Amy."

She swam.

Micah stroked behind her slightly to her right, protecting her. He could have easily passed her and reached the shore first, but he stayed behind making sure the caiman didn't catch up with her. She swam harder, reaching as far as she could with each stroke, making each pull through the mucky water count. Finally, she could put her feet on the bottom of the river; slogged through and flopped on the sandy edge looking behind her. The caiman had slunk away.

Micah collapsed beside her, breathing hard.

"*O senhor, senhorita,* are you all right?" Jonathas ran toward them, eyes wide with the horror of witnessing the events. First, Micah and the jeep, then the threat of the caiman.

Were they all right? Amy wasn't sure. "What just happened?" She reached up to wring the water from her hair, hands shaking violently. Micah stood, sloughed the wetness from his face and eyes and looked out over the water. The tail end of the jeep stuck up out of the river, but it was disappearing fast. "I'm not sure, but I don't think that was any accident."

David Ruibero, the chief of police, arrived about an hour later. Juan then called Lucas from the medical mission to come check out Amy, even though she insisted she was fine and that *he* was the one who needed checking out. Lucas confirmed her self-diagnosis, and Juan relaxed a little.

They gathered in the main building in the cafeteria where they sipped freshly brewed coffee and talked about the incident.

"I want that jeep hauled up and examined," Juan stated. "That was no accident. In order for it to drive so straight and right up the dock, the steering and the gas pedal had to have been jammed."

"Did you see anything, Jonathas?" Lucas asked.

"No, *senhor,* I'm sorry. I was taking care of the cows, and I heard the jeep start up. I chased it, but it was too fast and I could not keep up. I also couldn't see who was driving. I followed the tracks and got there in time to see the jeep going down the dock toward you." His voice choked, and he cleared his throat. "I thought you were dead."

The chief eyed the teenager suspiciously. "Are you sure about your story?"

Jonathas blinked, all sign of worry gone, his face now a blank facade. "Believe what you will. I do not lie."

David drew himself up, and a muscle twitched in his jaw. He kept himself under control with obvious effort. "I would appreciate your cooperation, not your disrespect."

Juan translated most of the conversation for Amy since it was all in Portuguese.

Jonathas calmed down, but not much. Instead, the sullen look Juan knew best slid over the teen's face. The chief said, "Well, if you happen to remember anything else, would you please get in touch with me? I can't catch a criminal I can't find."

"Right. Can I leave now? I still have chores to finish then I want to get ready for the picnic."

Juan slapped the boy on the back and thanked him. Jonathas left, and Lucas brought up another subject that Juan had been wondering about. "Have you gotten any information back about the darts?"

David nodded. "Yes. I was going to e-mail or call you, but when I got the call about this situation, I brought the report along." He reached in his back pocket and pulled out a paper, unfolded it and said, "The lab said that the tests they ran confirm that it's poison from the poison dart frog. If any of those tips had hit you, you would have been paralyzed. The poison affects the nervous system almost immediately. Very serious stuff."

Amy shuddered, the information and

damp clothes chilling her. Juan wrapped an arm around her shoulders. "So, what do we do now? That's three times someone's tried to kill me and I don't have a clue why. We need to find this person before he tries again and manages to succeed."

David said, "I'll have a truck get out here and see if we can get the jeep pulled out of the river. It could take a while."

Lucas piped in, "Tell them I'll double their hourly wage if they'll do it today."

The chief raised a brow, but didn't argue. Instead, he shrugged and said, "It's your money." He pulled out a satellite phone, punched in a number and walked off to make the arrangements.

Juan looked at Lucas. "Thanks."

"No problem."

Amy pulled away from him and said, "I'm going to change clothes and go tell Anna what's going on. Will you please let me know when you find something out about the jeep?"

Juan nodded. "Sure."

Amy left and Lucas asked, "I guess you didn't need me to set you up, huh?"

Amy still shook, her nerves snapping as she walked back toward the main building that housed Anna's office. She needed to talk to someone, or she'd burst. Hopefully, Anna had a few free moments and Amy could unload on her. Plus, she'd left her satellite phone plugged in and she needed to check it to see if anyone had called. She hadn't taken it down to the dock because she hadn't wanted to have any interruptions during her quiet time.

She sure hadn't counted on a runaway jeep for an interruption.

Upon reaching her room, she quickly showered and changed, then headed toward Anna's office to update the woman on the recent events.

The door to the temporary playroom swung open, and Amy stopped to see Carlita standing there still in her pajamas, her little stuffed bunny clutched in her left arm. When she saw Amy, her mouth form a perfect O and her eyes went wide.

Amy crouched down on the child's level, smiled and used her Portuguese to say, "Hello, Carlita. How are you this morning?"

Carlita gave a half smile, and Amy's heart leaped in her chest. More progress. "Are you looking for something? Someone?"

Carlita looked back over her shoulder, then back at Amy.

"Is Salvador with you?"

At her brother's name, Carlita's brown

eyes lightened, but she remained silent. Amy said, "Okay, will you take my hand and let's see if we can find him?"

The little girl hesitated, so Amy reassured her, "Come on, I'll help you find him."

Finally, hesitantly, Carlita held out a small brown hand, and Amy took it gently. The feel of the tiny fingers curling around her own made her feel like weeping. The little girl's trust was such a precious thing.

She decided to take care of Carlita, then track down Anna. They were almost there when Salvador emerged from the room on the right, dressed haphazardly and toweling his short hair.

He spotted them coming toward him and stopped, staring at their clasped hands. In English he said, "There you are. I took a shower, and when I came out, she was gone. Thank you for bringing her back."

"You're welcome. I ran into her on my way to see Anna. I think this one was looking for you. She's such a sweet girl." Amy squeezed the small hand still in hers. "I hope she's beginning to like me a little."

Salvador shot her a tight smile and said, "Yes, she needs a woman, a *mamãe*." Almost to himself, he added, "It was *wrong* what happened. So wrong. My family should not be dead. She misses . . ." He looked away.

Amy hurt for him and reached out to pat his bony shoulder. Amy couldn't help notice the anger, the boiling rage that simmered just beneath the surface at the injustice his family had suffered. Hopefully, the love and care he received at the orphanage would make a difference in his future. She certainly admired his dedication to Carlita.

"You're right. It was wrong. I don't know why God allows things like that to happen, but try to lean on Him, Salvador."

He shook his head, taking his sister's hand in his. "I pray every day, believe me. I pray for the men who . . ."

"Who what?"

"Nothing . . . forget it."

"Salvador, I . . ." What could she say? Maybe Micah could talk to him. Man to man. They'd each suffered tragedy in their lives. Perhaps Micah could help. Making a mental note to ask Micah to talk to him, she changed the subject. "Well, here is little Carlita, safe and sound. I'm looking for Anna. Have you seen her?"

Salvador nodded toward the hall. "She is in her office, I believe."

"Thanks."

Amy waved and little Carlita waved back. She walked on past Salvador and Carlita's room to the office at the end of the hall.

Anna had taken over running the orphanage after Cassidy's kidnapping.

She knocked on the door.

"Come in."

Amy stepped in. "Hey there. I just stopped by to let you know someone tried to kill Micah again, and I happened to be there this time."

Anna stilled, "Micah?"

Amy's hand flew to her mouth. "Did I say Micah? I meant Juan."

Eyes narrowed, Anna said, "You wouldn't mean Micah McKnight, would you? Because I know all about *that* Micah. Cassidy told me about her brother when she was here getting to know Alexis. Why did you call Juan Micah?"

Amy blew out a sigh. She'd been coming to spill her guts anyway, so she might as well start with the subject of Micah. "Juan *is* Micah McKnight."

Anna sat in her chair with a thump. "What makes you say that?"

"The birthmark on his stomach and back. I saw it the other day when we were hurrying through the jungle. A branch ripped his shirt almost completely off and . . . there it was. It looks like half of a belt wrapped around his waist. I used to tease him about it all the time."

"Have you told him?"

Amy shook her head. "No. I mean, what do I say? How do I tell him? He doesn't remember anything. Would it hurt him for me to try to jar his memory? And if I tell him who *he* is, I have to tell him who *I* am and who my *mother* is and what she did to him . . ." Amy sucked in a much needed breath.

"I see your dilemma, but, Amy, you've got to tell him. Because if you don't and he remembers . . ."

Amy groaned and dropped her face into her hands, "I know," she said through her fingers, "but I don't know how to approach it. I mean, medically . . ."

"I'm pretty sure it won't hurt him," Lucas spoke from the doorway. The two women looked at him. "Sorry, I didn't mean to eavesdrop, I was just coming to check on you, Amy, and see how you were feeling after your dunking in the river. I heard you talking." He shrugged. "I probably listened longer than I had to, but you were discussing my patient . . . and friend." He didn't seem terribly embarrassed about listening in, just honest and concerned. "You can tell him who he is, just ease into it. As far as I know, there's no medical reason he's blocking his memories. Knowing his identity may actually help him recover faster."

Anna bit her lip. Amy averted her eyes and said, "You don't know the whole story, Lucas. I'm afraid of what he'll do if I tell him everything."

"So tell me."

Amy shook her head. "No, I . . . I can't. I'm sorry."

Lucas shrugged. "Well, even if you don't want to confide in me, you need to tell Juan . . . er, Micah who he is."

"I've called his family, hoping to tell them and see what they want to do, but they're on an extended cruise. They'll be gone for another week or so. I've left messages for them to call me on every number I could remember. So far, nothing. I haven't checked my phone today, but I'm not holding out hope. They're not expecting to hear anything from or about Micah, so . . ." She gave a sad laugh. "They've finally accepted that he's not coming home and now . . ." She hiccupped a soft sob. "Now I've run across him and don't have a clue what to do about it."

"Tell him. Just be gentle in how you do it," Lucas insisted.

Amy nodded and glanced at Anna. "Okay, you're right. He needs to know. And I suppose I should be the one to tell him." She closed her eyes against the thought. She really didn't want to do it.

Lucas said, "He's having flashes of memory anyway. He may remember on his own before you get a chance to tell him."

"I'll tell him . . . after the picnic."

She slipped back to her room, stopping just inside the door. Spying a note on her pillow, she picked it up and read the broken English.

"Come to bar in town, named Tefe Nights. Meet at back entrance tomorrow night, eight o'clock. I know how to find Maria Morales. Will tell you for five thousand American dollars."

Six

Juan slammed a fist into the wall and winced. Rubbing the bruised flesh, he decided that was a dumb thing to do. All he needed was a broken hand. But frustration had him in its grip and wasn't letting go. *Who's trying to kill me? And why? What have I done to make someone so angry with me?*

Another thought struck him. Did someone know who he was? Before his amnesia days, did he have an enemy that he couldn't remember — but one who obviously remembered him?

He racked his brain trying to think. Okay, he'd been with Lucas in the gym the first time someone had tried to kill him, then on the dock the second time. Both times Amy had shown up after the fact. And Jonathas had been there both times — after the incident.

Most likely, Jonathas would know how to make poison darts, but what possible reason could the boy have to want to kill him?

Amy had probably watched enough movies and television to know how to jam a gas pedal and steering wheel, but how would she have been able to set everything up so fast? She'd been with him only moments before the incident. Unless she'd had help. But why would she have rushed into the river to look for him if she'd just tried to kill him? And why would she have tried to smother him with a pillow only to do CPR and bring him back from the dead?

Then he pictured her sitting on the end of the dock with her Bible. While she'd been troubled, there had also been a quiet peace surrounding her. No, it wasn't Amy, of that he had no doubt. And he really didn't think it could be Jonathas. But if not one of them, then who? And again . . . why?

Argh. He was going to go nuts. After a quick shower and change of clothes, he felt much better. A little tired, but that was nothing unusual, especially on days when he overdid it. Almost getting killed could probably be considered overdoing it.

He decided to go check out the picnic first, then see if Amy wanted to help him work on the wing later. He'd even offer to share his tool belt. He grinned to himself . . . then frowned. Why was he seeking her out?

He'd be better off leaving her alone, yet he felt pulled to her. She fascinated him with her deep faith, bright smile and sometimes sad eyes. Her unwavering care for him when he'd been sick had touched him. Sure, she'd lost her patience with him a couple of times, but she'd never yelled at him or forced an issue; she just let him figure out on his own that she was right.

And Lucas was right about her eyes. They held pain from something. Something she was either running from or trying to ignore. Juan sighed. He had enough problems without borrowing anyone else's. And yet . . .

Mentally smacking himself upside the head, he ordered, *Leave her alone, man. She's not for you. At least not until you figure out who you are.*

His stomach finally claimed his attention, and the picnic was waiting — hopefully, so was Amy. He opened the door to leave and stopped. The memories were back. The images all ran together in his mind as he struggled to sort them out.

A large house, a mansion, with a swimming pool. Cooking out on a grill, laughing with friends, people — family? Doing a cannonball into the deep end of the pool. A redhead ran up and threw her arms around him to give him a hug. His mother — he didn't know how he knew the woman was his mother, he just did — shook her finger at him and ordered him, "You need to find another job. It's just too dangerous. It's going to get you killed one day."

His job? He ignored the thought, not wanting to disrupt the memories.

A tall distinguished man laughed and crooked an elbow around his neck. "Son, you do what you've got to do. Right now, we're just glad you're here. Welcome home."

He blinked.

God? I don't know if I have the same kind of relationship with You that Amy has, but I know I need some help here. If You're listening, let me figure out who's trying to kill me.

He continued on out the door, down the hall and turned right. As he approached Anna's office, he heard voices.

"I wouldn't ask you if it wasn't important," Amy was saying.

Not wanting to eavesdrop, Juan knocked on the door. Two heads swiveled as one. Amy's eyes lightened and relief spread across her face. She asked, "Hey there, how are you?"

Juan answered, "Hungry. Aren't you going to the picnic?" He asked the question of both ladies, but his eyes were on Amy. The women glanced at each other and Amy nodded affirmatively.

Anna said, "Yes, just as soon as I finish up some paperwork. Why don't you and Amy head down to the ball field? She and I can finish this discussion later."

Juan wondered at the pointed look Anna sent Amy, but didn't figure it was any of his business . . . although he had to admit to his curiosity. Well, she'd tell him if she wanted to.

Amy smiled, but Juan thought it looked strained. She said, "All right, I'm a little hungry. Why not?"

Juan felt his heart start thudding and told it to stop. It was a picnic lunch. That was all.

The fun was in full swing when they arrived at the field. Picnic tables groaned under the weight of goodies that would tempt even the strongest dieter. And Juan wasn't on a diet. His stomach growled again, earning a glance and a laugh from Amy. "Hungry?"

"Starved."

"Come on, it looks as if almost everyone has already gone through the line."

Juan followed her over to the spread and grabbed a paper plate. He started filling it up, then subtly glanced around, wondering if whoever was after him was here. Was it one of the staff? The grounds crew? And why? What was it about him that made someone want to kill him?

Amy caught his attention as she moved to find a place to sit. She moved with a supple, natural grace that most women would envy or practice endlessly to achieve. Yet the lines between her brows spoke of something on her mind.

They found a seat on a checkered blanket that provided a front-row view of all the activities going on in and around the ball field. As Juan sat down opposite her, he asked, "What's wrong?"

She looked startled. "Why do you ask that?"

"Call it intuition."

"I just have a lot on my mind," she said as she blew out a sigh. "Look, this may not be the best timing and I was going to wait until after the picnic to tell you, but I . . ."

"Hi, do you mind if I join you?" Jonathas asked, a camera swinging around his neck.

Juan mentally groaned at the interruption, but smiled up at the teen waiting beside the blanket, plate in hand. "Sure, have a seat." He pointed to the camera. "So, are you the official picnic photographer?"

"Looks like it." He shrugged. "I don't

mind. It's kind of a hobby of mine anyway. Anna gave me the equipment and told me to go to work." He laughed and lifted the camera. "Smile."

Juan grabbed Amy and pulled her close. Her clean, sweet scent made his head swim, but he managed to grin at the camera even as he enjoyed her closeness.

The picture taken, Jonathas sat back. Amy asked, "How are you handling this morning?"

Jonathas blew out a breath, his laughter fading. Juan wished she'd left it alone, but could tell she'd asked out of sincere concern. "I don't know what happened. One minute I was taking care of the cows, the next the jeep was driving down the road."

Juan leaned in closer. Might as well take the opportunity to find out what he could. "Do you think someone followed you out there?"

"It's possible," Jonathas said around a bite of salad. "I wasn't driving fast, and I always go around the same time every morning. Today, I was a little later than usual, but not too much."

Amy nodded, "I don't normally see you leave."

"*Sim,* I know." Jonathas looked at Juan. "You have made someone very mad. What have you done?"

"I wish I knew, Jonathas. I wish I knew."

Amy crunched on a homemade potato chip and studied the crowd, her nerves unsettled. She felt watched, as if eyes followed her every move, but she couldn't figure out why.

Several laughing, giggling children played on a makeshift waterslide. One of the relief workers squirted soap on the plastic to make it a faster ride. A young teenage girl got a running start and went headfirst down the sloping hill where spectators normally gathered to watch the baseball games. Today, it was the perfect place for a water slide. Her high-pitched scream brought a laugh to the other workers supervising the activity.

There was a dunking booth, a face-painting area, a pie-eating contest and other games adapted from the United States. The outer part of the ball field had been set up for a dodgeball game.

Amy had come to love the game, but today her heart wasn't into playing. Keeping her senses attuned to the people around her, in case one of them was a killer ready to strike again, and trying to work up the courage to tell Micah his identity took all her energy. She was sure once he remembered her, he wouldn't want anything to do with her. He'd only known her as a spoiled socialite, interested in shopping and partying. But not telling him was selfish, and she couldn't put it off any longer.

She'd definitely tell him tonight.

"Hey, you want to play?" he said, interrupting her thoughts.

The half smile on his face drew an answering smile from her. "Nah. Why? Do you want to?"

"Looks kinda fun."

Jonathas laughed. "It's a great game. Come on."

Giving in to the pressure, Amy grabbed Micah's outstretched hand, allowing him to pull her to her feet. She could get used to the feel of his hand in hers. Easily. He held it as they jogged over to the field where the game was just getting started. Amy and Micah ended up on opposite teams. Jonathas stood beside her. Their teammate on the other end of the field lobbed the ball over the opposing team. The ball headed straight for Amy. She dodged it.

The child on the other side caught it, then reared back and let loose with a ball that beaned a young boy about nine years old in the shoulder. He gave a good-natured shrug on his way off the field.

The other team picked up the ball and tossed it back toward Amy's team. Everyone scattered, letting the ball roll away. This time, Amy picked it up and, without hesitating, zinged it straight for Micah. It caught him smack in the stomach. The look of surprise sent her into gales of laughter. Then she felt the ball punch her lightly in the thigh. She was out. It wasn't exactly American dodgeball, but it was fun.

This time Micah was laughing. "That'll teach you to laugh at me."

A snicker escaped from her. "It was worth it. You should have seen the look on your face."

"Where'd you learn to throw like that?"

Immediately sadness replaced giddiness. Two and a half years ago, he would have never had to ask that question. He would have known. Smiling up at him, she hid the momentary twinge. "I was the pitcher on my high-school softball team. I had to sneak out to play." She took a deep breath, decided to take a chance and said in a snooty voice, "My mother, Cecelia Graham, wife of Senator Graham, did not deem softball a sport worthy of her only daughter." In her normal voice, she said, "Now, if I'd chosen ice-skating or an equestrian sport, that would have been all well and good."

Micah took her hand again. "Your mother sounds like quite the character. Come on, let's go get some dessert."

Unfortunately, Micah had shown no recognition of her mother's name. *Quite the character.* Yes, that was one way of putting it. Amy shoved the bitterness aside and felt a chill raise the hair on her neck. Subtly looking around, she noticed nothing out of place. Just fun and games. Why was she feeling so skittish? Doing her best to ignore the creepy sensations, yet staying alert for any suspicious activity, she followed Micah back to their spot.

Jonathas ended up walking back with them. Sitting on the blanket, Amy eyed her watch. She was running out of time. Soon, the picnic would be over and she'd need to have that talk with Micah.

Goose bumps danced along her nerve ends. She looked around, searching the familiar faces of each of the staff. Who held something against Micah? Who'd tried to kill him three times? And when would he or she strike again? Maybe here at the picnic? At that thought, she wondered if Micah should have stayed away. Would his presence here be a threat to the safety of the others? Or should they have simply asked for extra security to be available? Micah was obviously the target. Surely, no one would try anything with this crowd. She shuddered and prayed the person would just keep his or her distance. Just knowing that someone was out there put a damper on the afternoon. That, and the fact that she had to tell Micah who he was.

Looking up, she saw Salvador working, cleaning up in the aftermath of the picnic. Anna had said she offered him the day off, encouraging him to join in the fun, but he'd refused, not wanting to give up the day's wages. Amy watched him wipe down the picnic tables and empty the trash into a plastic tub. He seemed to take pride in his work.

Occasionally, he would look up and watch them talking. Amy smiled at him and he nodded. Carlita wandered into the area, spied Amy and made a beeline toward her. The little girl tapped Amy's leg, as though asking permission to sit in her lap. Shock, then joy, zipped through Amy at the overture of affection, and she pulled the child up into her arms.

Salvador stopped cleaning, and his eyes went wide. Shocked him, too, apparently. Carlita snuggled her bunny under her chin and laid her head on Amy's shoulder. Within minutes, she was asleep. She acted a lot younger than six years old, most likely due to the trauma she'd endured.

Micah's eyes followed the movements, his eyes crinkling at the corners when he offered Amy a grin. "Seems you've made a friend."

Amy kissed the silky dark head, her throat tight with emotion for the pain this child had been through — was still going through. "She misses her mama. Guess I'll do for right now. I still think it would be a good idea for her to see a child psychologist."

Jonathas shook his head. "It is a shame."

Amy asked, "What?"

"How her family died."

Amy frowned, glanced at Micah and noticed the same expression on his face. "What do you mean?"

Jonathas glanced over at Salvador, who had resumed his duties.

With a lowered voice, he explained in English, "The human traffickers came, tried to take the older girl, Natalia. The parents fought back, so the men killed them. Took the girl anyway. Shot up anyone they could find, even the baby, then set the house on fire. Salvador was coming home from the store with Carlita when he saw the flames. When he realized what was happening, he took Carlita and ran to hide in the jungle.

He told me this a couple of days ago. Carlita is all he has left in the world."

The tears on her lashes threatened to fall, but Amy blinked them back and cleared her throat. She'd known his family had been killed but hadn't been aware of the details. "That's awful," she whispered.

"Yes, there are some very awful people who live here." Jonathas's eyes hardened. "My own father was one of them. Even though he is dead now, I still carry hate for him in my heart. And for a lot of other people, too. I do not like the hate, but it is there." Jonathas snickered, a humorless sound. "It would make him proud if he had lived, my father. The one thing I never wanted to do. Make him proud."

Micah said, "What? I didn't know you felt that way. Why? Who was your father?"

Jonathas just shook his head and picked up the remains of his lunch. "Very bad man. Very bad."

After he left, Amy looked at Micah and said, "There's so much hurt here. How do you help them all?"

Micah looked at Carlita, snoozing on Amy's lap, and said, "Like that, I guess. Love them one at a time."

"Come on, Juan, we need you in the dunking booth!" Anna called from the event. Carlita woke at the shout, blinking and rubbing her eyes.

"Oh, no." He held up his hands. "You get me in that booth and I'll never get out."

Amy shoved his shoulder. "Ah, go on. Be a good sport."

Several children ran over to him, latching on to his hands and legs. "Juan, Juan, Juan," they chanted.

Giving a rueful laugh, he rose, allowing himself to be escorted to the booth. Amy followed them, a grin on her face, Carlita's hand tucked in hers. Oh, boy, no way was she missing this one. Looking back over his shoulder, Juan narrowed his eyes. "You're not planning on participating in this, are you?"

A smile threatened to break loose. She bit her lip, widening her eyes innocently. "Why, whatever do you mean?"

"You wouldn't," he growled as he climbed the few steps to the platform settling himself on the collapsible seat.

"Wouldn't what?" Sweetness dripped from her tone. She eyed the bull's-eye sticking out to the side. Chills scooted up her spine. There was that watched feeling again. She stopped, turned and looked for . . . something. All she saw were the grinning, expect-ant faces of the crowd gathered to cheer her on. She shrugged off the feeling. Who would try something with this group?

She focused back on Micah. "You know what," he was saying. "Drop the innocent act. You're already warming up that pitching arm, aren't you?"

Flexing the fingers of her pitching hand, Amy loosened it up. She shook off the creepy feeling and forced a wicked smile. She felt someone place a ball in her hand. "I think it's time for a swim, don't you?"

"Amy . . ." he warned.

"I'm sorry," she snickered, getting into the fun of teasing him. "This is just too good an opportunity to pass up."

"You realize if you do this, you open yourself up to all kinds of possible, unexpected moments of revenge on my part, don't you?"

She pretended to think about it for a moment. "Yeah, but I think it's worth it." The audience cheered. She drew back her arm. Micah glared at her, but she could see the hint of laughter behind the look. He was enjoying this as much as she. Releasing the ball, she watched as it skimmed the target and fell to the ground.

A groan sounded all around. Micah shifted on the seat, gave her a taunting look, but kept his mouth shut. She grabbed another ball, wound up and let it fly. It went wide to the chorus of another round of disappointed mutters.

Tilting his head, Micah gave her a mocking smile. "What's the matter, you got pitcher's elbow or something?"

Insulted, Amy said, "Well, I wasn't going to do it, but you asked for it. Ready or not, hold your breath." The last ball flew from her fingers, smacked the bull's-eye dead in the center. The explosion that followed rocked Amy and the onlookers to the core.

Screaming cries resounded through his shocked mind right before the water closed over him and the booth fell apart. He felt himself falling, hitting the soggy ground; pain lanced through him, grabbing his right side. Flames flickered, licked around him. Sudden memories flooded his mind even as he fought his way out of the debris.

"Something's wrong, it doesn't feel right," he whispered into the microphone, then reached up and shoved the earpiece a little tighter into his ear canal.

"Then get out now," came the order.

He gripped the boy's hand, turned to repeat the words to the three men behind him. Before he could open his mouth, the explosion threw him backward to slam into the stone fireplace, his head cracking against the edge. Pain swirled, his world blurred. Fighting for consciousness, he pulled the small body closer, wincing as the four-year-old screamed his terror.

Get us out of here, God. Please get us out of here.

They'd been set up.

Betrayed.

Darkness closed in fast. Another explosion shook the building even as it crumbled around him.

Hands pulled him from the debris. Amy sobbed over him. "Are you okay? Talk to me, please tell me you're okay."

Ringing ears, his spinning head and the pain in his right side made it hard to focus. Was anyone else hurt? He felt himself lifted, carried a short distance, then settled on a soft bed.

"Lucas is on the way."

"I thought he was coming to the picnic." Amy's voice ricocheted through his head.

"He had an emergency."

"Hey, I'm okay," he whispered. His left hand felt heavy, bruised and throbbing. His right side felt as if it were on fire. Amy touched the side of his face, tears shimmered, threatening to spill over the edge. He stared up at her, grateful for her concern, her worry, but wanting to reassure her that it wasn't necessary.

"What's going on here?"

The chief of police. How had he gotten here so quickly?

"David, thank you for coming so fast." Anna's voice. "You must have been close."

"I was." Short, sweet and to the point. The man offered no explanation. "What happened?"

"The dunking booth blew up," Juan rasped. His mind was starting to clear, the shock wearing off as the ringing in his ears settled. He pulled himself into a sitting position, gasping as the fire turned into an inferno in his right side. Focusing on Amy's blue gaze, he asked, "Was anyone else hurt?"

"Some cuts and bruises, but you took the brunt of it," Amy's voice shook. "You scared me to death."

"Let me go take a look," David said. Anna led him from the room to show him the way to the mangled booth.

Amy leaned her head against his shoulder. "I'm so sorry."

He gave a small laugh, then winced as fire shot through his side. "What for? You didn't blow up the booth."

"No, not technically. I was just the tool." She looked up into his eyes. "You could have been killed."

"Again."

"It was some kind of homemade mini-bomb." David Ruibero's voice cut into the conversation as he flipped over the device that looked like old-fashioned dynamite taped together with duct tape. "It was a remote-control deal." Looking at Micah, he said, "There's no doubt someone wants you dead — and he knew you'd be up in that booth. There were two of these. I defused this one. The one bomb that went off was actually on the far end of the booth, underneath it. The only way I can figure you survived was that the location and force of the bomb caused an almost ejection-type explosion that caused you to be thrown out and into the air in the opposite direction of the falling booth. You had a hard landing, but at least you still have all your limbs. You're lucky this one didn't explode when the other one did. I think one of the wires must have dislodged itself. If this one had gone off, too, you wouldn't be here with us."

"Yeah." Juan touched his side, it felt as if he had cracked a rib or something. "Lucky me."

Lucas entered the area. "What's going on?" He looked at Juan. "You again? Good grief, man, I'm going to have to start charging you double."

Juan grimaced. "Very funny. We both know what double of nothing is."

"Let me see that side."

Amy moved aside, concern drawing her eyebrows down, but she bit her lip and kept quiet.

Lucas ended up declaring Juan fine except for a possible cracked rib, but most likely a bruised one, and a sprained hand. He was very lucky, the doctor stated, shaking his head, while taping up Juan's ribs. "You need to come in for an X-ray."

"Just tape them tight. If it's cracked, it's cracked. Either way, the treatment's the same."

Sighing, Lucas asked, "Are you sure you aren't a cat disguised as a human? You've got more lives than anyone I've ever come across."

"You're just the comedian today, aren't you?"

"I gotta laugh, buddy, because something tells me unless you catch this person who's causing all these problems, I'm going to be crying at your funeral."

Amy caught up with Lucas just as he was getting into his car. "Lucas, wait."

"Something wrong?" Concern etched his handsome features, but Amy's mind was totally on one man.

"I haven't told Micah who he is, yet. I was going to tell him tonight, but now . . ."

Lucas blew out a sigh. "Why don't you wait a couple of days, just until he's feeling a little better physically. I gave him some pain medication, so he'll probably be out for the rest of the night anyway. I really thought he'd remember on his own by now and he still could, given time, but I know he'd really appreciate you telling him."

Amy didn't think Micah would feel grateful at all, probably more like incensed that she'd waited. She sighed, keeping that thought to herself. "Okay. I'll tell him as soon as he's recovered a bit. Thanks, Lucas."

"See you later."

Amy watched him drive off, relieved for the short reprieve, yet frustrated, too. She'd worked up the nerve to tell him, but now there was a delay. But she would tell him and soon.

The next afternoon, feeling sore, but incredibly grateful to be alive, Juan was back out working on the building against the advice of everyone around him. Finally giving in to

111

pain and the wisdom of resting his rib, he headed back inside. On his way back to his room, he came across Amy and Anna in the hallway outside her office. The two were in a heated debate about something, and Juan wondered if he should keep going or find another route.

As he was trying to decide, Amy said, "I have to go, Anna. Just keep your phone on in case I need some help, okay?" Before Anna could answer or Juan could make his presence known, Amy darted away. Juan clenched his jaw. She was still hiding something, keeping her secrets. It hurt because he thought they'd grown close enough for her to trust him with whatever it was that she needed help with. Enough was enough. What would she need help with? One way to find out. "Anna?"

She turned. Relief flickered briefly in her eyes, then indecision. "Hello, Juan. How are you feeling?"

Her voice sounded forced, stilted, as if she were trying to make conversation while her mind worked on a problem.

"Sore and a little banged up, but otherwise fine. What's wrong, Anna?"

She bit her lip. An unusual action for this strong woman who seemed unflappable.

He frowned at her. "What's Amy doing

that's got you worried? Why would she need some help?"

Her eyes flickered, then she gave in and said, "Come into my office and I'll tell you . . . but only because I *am* worried."

Juan followed her into the office to stand just inside the door. He ignored the sound of a horn honking, but at the sound, Anna flew to the window and gasped. "She's really doing it. She must have called that taxi two hours ago." She whirled around to face him. "I hate to do this to you, but do you feel up to following Amy? She's going in to Tefe to meet someone and wouldn't tell me who, but I get the feeling it's a dangerous situation. She asked me to keep my satellite phone on in case she needed me. But if she really needs help, my answering the phone isn't going to do much good. She needs someone with her. I'd ask Romero, but he went over to the medical mission to meet Lucas about something."

Juan narrowed his eyes, focusing on one word. "Dangerous?"

Anna shrugged. "I don't know, it's just a feeling. What I do know is that she's looking for someone whose reputation spells danger. Please, go, before she gets too far ahead of you. Take the new jeep. It's gassed and ready to go."

Instead of asking why Amy hadn't taken the jeep herself, he grabbed the keys from Anna and raced from the building. A sense of urgency pushed him and he found himself praying protection for Amy — and himself.

Amy rode with concentrated silence. She prayed nonstop, asking God to look over her and keep her out of any danger. She honestly didn't believe anything was going to happen, but no sense going in unarmed. *Therefore, put on the full armor of God, that you may stand strong in the day of evil. For our struggle is not against flesh and blood, but against the powers of evil in this present darkness.* The verse from Ephesians chapter six ran through her mind endlessly. Amy knew that what she was doing was probably stupid, and yet she could no more stop herself from going than she could stop breathing. Anna promised to keep her satellite phone on, and Amy had hers fully charged. She'd paid careful attention to that since leaving messages for the McKnights to call her.

She should have asked Micah to come with her. But she didn't want to chance putting him in danger, especially not now with him still suffering from his latest brush with death. Also, she'd have to explain why she needed him, which meant telling him about her mother, which also meant when he remembered who he was, he'd know immediately who she was and what her mother had done to him. She'd planned to tell Micah who he was yesterday after the picnic, but then the explosion had happened and Lucas told her to wait.

Tomorrow, she promised, she'd tell him first thing. Assuming she made it to tomorrow. *Please, God.*

The taxi screeched to a halt, and Amy pulled the money from the back pocket of her jeans. She'd not bothered bringing a purse. No sense in tempting a criminal. Her satellite phone rested snuggly in her other back pocket, and she'd set it to vibrate. No way was she going to end up like one of those dumb chicks in the movies who carried their cell phone to a rendezvous only to have it ring at an inopportune moment.

Of course, she told herself, she was exactly like one of those dumb chicks in the movies who went to meet the bad guy without taking along backup. Amy refused to think about that, reassuring herself that Anna knew where she was and had her phone at hand. Reinforcements were just a button away, and the police department was four blocks south.

Climbing out of the taxi, she watched it drive away and wondered if she should have asked the driver to wait. No, she decided, she had the company number; she'd call another one when she was ready to leave.

Looking around, she shuddered. Ugh. Not the nice part of town, obviously. Slowly, she approached the bar. Even when she'd been a partyer back before she'd turned to God, she'd never frequented the sleazy bars, only the high-class ones — if there was such a thing. But this . . . *Jesus, I really need you right now.*

Darkness had fallen about an hour and a half ago. Dim streetlights led her around the side of the building to the back of the bar where she'd been instructed to go. She stepped slowly, scanning the alley, left then right. Filth lined the area, and she shuddered at the odor of decay, spoiled food and who knew what else.

Her heart pounded, shivers of fear crawled up and down her spine and the hair on her nape stood straight out. She choked down her need to gag as her breathing grew shallow, panting. Nope, this was a very bad idea. *I need to leave, don't I, God?* Listening to her little inner voice, she spun on her heel, crunching the refuse underfoot as she headed to the entrance of the bar. She'd stand under the brightest streetlamp she could find and call for another taxi.

Behind her, a scrape. She whirled back. Saw nothing. Fear licked along her veins until she thought she'd spontaneously combust. She prayed, claiming God's promise of protection.

"Maria?" she said softly.

The arm was around her throat before she could blink; the hand across her mouth before she could release the scream trapped in her throat. Her hands flew to grasp her captor's forearms, his foul body odor mingling with the scent of the rotting garbage.

"What do you want with Maria?" the voice was low, menacing.

Amy shivered, fought the fear, tried to answer, but the hand cut off any sound she might make. She grabbed at it and it loosened. Gasping, she said, "I need to speak with her. I have some questions for her."

"Leave Maria alone. Do not look for her. If you do, you may find yourself dead, *entenda?*"

Fear smothered her, weakness hit her knees and she struggled to stay upright, not sag against the man behind her. "Please, you don't understand. Just tell her I want to speak with her. I'm not here to find her to claim any reward or to lead the authorities to her. I just need to talk to her. Just talk. That's all."

A knife appeared, the arm tightened across her throat. Amy felt the blackness falling over her. She wheezed, "Maria's my grandmother." The arm around her neck jerked, the hand around the knife paused.

And then she was free. She sank to the ground, panting, sucking in air to oxygen-deprived lungs. Trembling seized her, and she shook as though afflicted with palsy.

A scuffle behind her drew her attention, and she saw two men slugging it out. Her captor slid under a light briefly allowing her to catch a glimpse of his round face. The policeman from the other day. Roberto! The man who'd walked in on her talking to the chief and threatened her.

Her rescuer clipped him on the chin and he stumbled, went down, scrabbled away on all fours. Light cut across the second man's face and Amy gasped.

Micah!

How had he found her? He had the policeman pinned against the wall. Fist clenched, Micah drew his arm back to deliver another punch and Amy screamed, "No, let him go."

Micah turned to her, caught off guard at her shriek. The other man shoved his hands against Micah's chest, throwing him off balance, and then slipped away, vanishing in the shadows. Obviously torn between wanting to go after the guy and the desire to check on Amy, he hesitated, pressed a hand to his side and limped to where Amy still sat, her legs unable to hold her weight.

He stooped down and grabbed her by the arms, wincing in pain as he hefted her up. His breath came in short puffs, his words through gritted teeth. "What. Do. You. Think. You. Are. Doing?"

Amy threw her arms around his neck and hung on tight. Sobs broke through, and she let them all out onto Micah's unsuspecting shoulder.

SEVEN

Juan held her as she wept. His rib throbbed unmercifully, his hand likewise. Punching her attacker with a sprained hand hadn't been the best idea, but he'd been short of options. Out of fear for her, he felt like shaking her, but didn't figure that would help. One meltdown was enough for the night. Patting her shoulder with his right hand, he said, "Come on. Let's get over to the police department and report this."

Amy pulled away, scrubbing her eyes and shaking her head. "No, I don't want to report it. I'm fine. No one got hurt, so let's just go back to the orphanage and forget this ever happened."

Juan snorted. "Not likely. Now do you want to do it or shall I?"

"I said I'm not reporting it," Amy insisted angrily. "Just . . . trust me on this, okay?" But she would call the chief and tell him he had a traitor on his force. Although, without going into an explanation of how she knew this, he'd probably ignore her. Indecision warred within her. *Oh, God, tell me what to do!*

"Give me a reason. Secrets are not a good thing. They can get you killed." Why those words popped out his mouth, he had no idea, but she blanched and went white, so he assumed they hit home.

"No one knows that better than I do," she whispered.

Juan narrowed his eyes. "Okay, you don't want to let the police in on this little adventure. I guess it's understandable that you might consider the report a waste of time, but do you mind clueing me in?"

"Look, I appreciate you helping me out. But . . ." She frowned. "Wait a minute. How did you know I needed help?"

"A little birdie told me."

"A little birdie named Anna?"

He shrugged.

She sighed, rubbed the spot above her left eye as though it ached. "I'm . . . looking for someone. Someone who doesn't want to be found."

Eyes narrowed, he studied her face. A partial truth. "Who?"

"I'd rather not say."

His jaw clenched. "Fine." Stubborn

woman. He could tell she was on the verge of another meltdown, so he quit pushing. There would be time for that later. "Are you ready to get in the jeep?"

She nodded, wearily accepting his grudgingly offered hand.

Even as he pulled her to the jeep, his jaw clenched against the pain each step sent rushing through his body. He wondered how she'd managed to land herself in so much trouble. Who was she looking for? Why did that person think that Amy was a threat?

Without another word, he opened the door for her, then shut it behind her. Walking around to the driver's side, he crawled in and kept his silence. He'd let her be the next one to speak. He'd also let her actions sink in as they drove home.

Four minutes later, she asked, "Why can't I stop shaking? M-m-my teeth won't stop ch-ch-chattering."

Even though he knew he'd sweat bullets, he flipped the heater on high. She was in shock and as mad as he was with her for being so careless with her life, he had to do what he could to help her feel better. "You'll warm up in a minute."

"Th-thank you. That was a really dumb thing to do, wasn't it?"

"I hope you're not expecting me to dis-agree."

She was getting her wits back. "No, I guess not. I'd better call Anna and let her know I'm okay."

Juan focused on the drive back to the orphanage while Amy assured and reassured Anna that no harm had come to her, thanks to Juan's quick actions. She flipped the phone closed and leaned her head back against the leather seat. The jeep hummed along nicely, even though it bounced often on the pitted road.

"Nice jeep," he said.

Amy shrugged. "It seemed the least I could do."

"Why's that?"

Eyes still closed, she asked, "Do you remember anything at all? About who you are? Anything about your past?"

He glanced over at her. Why was she asking? "I have flashes. But the problem is, sometimes I'm not sure if they're truly memories or just wishes."

"What do you mean?"

Tense fingers clenched around the steer-ing wheel. Did he really want to tell her? Confide in her? After she'd cut him off and refused to tell him about what she was do-ing messing in dangerous business tonight?

He gave a mental shrug. Why not? Maybe if he opened himself up a little, she'd do the same. "I get these . . . movie trailers, I guess would be the best way to describe them. They come without warning, sometimes in my dreams. Other times I'm awake and they just hit me. Like today. I had a clip of what I thought was a memory, but I'm just not sure it's real."

Her eyes came open at that statement. "Why?"

"It was really weird. I was at this huge house, a mansion, and we were having some kind of pool party, a cookout and my family was there. At least I think they were my family. And then a helicopter landed. Everyone was really glad to see each other and we all had a great time swimming, joking around. You know. Anyway, I'm afraid that because I want something so bad, I'm forcing my mind to . . . play tricks . . . or something."

"Oh." The sound was a whisper.

He gave a self-conscious laugh. "I know, like I said, weird." He shook his head. "I'm just questioning everything going on in my head and it's making me crazy."

Her satellite phone vibrated, indicating a missed call. She hadn't felt it vibrate with the actual call. Of course she had been otherwise occupied for the last half hour or so. Looking at the screen, she groaned.

Cassidy. Oh, boy. She had to get to a place to call the woman back. But she was in a place where she could tell Micah a few things . . . like his name. It was time to do some serious explaining. "Okay, so . . . I need to . . . um . . . tell you some things."

He flicked a glance at her, then back to the road. "How about starting with what you were doing meeting scum all by your-self?" His phone rang and with a sigh, he held up a hand. "Hold on a minute. My turn." He pulled it out, opened it, listened intently for a few moments, then closed it. "That was the chief. He couldn't find any fingerprints on the bomb. He thinks who-ever built it wore gloves."

Amy blew out a breath, momentarily distracted. "Great. There're latex gloves all over the orphanage for staff in case of emergencies, cleaning up after meals, in the health center, you name it. Now what?"

"Now, you hold on to whatever it is you were going to tell me, go inside and let Anna know you're okay, then we'll talk tomorrow, okay? You're beat." He trailed a finger along her jaw causing her adrenaline to kick in for the second time that night. Only this time it definitely wasn't from terror.

His lips quirked in that smile that she remembered, and her heart shook with the fullness of her own memories. She remembered the pool party he'd told her he'd dreamed about. It had been to welcome him home on an extended leave from the Navy. Amy had looked forward to that day forever. She and her family had been on vacation in California, and Amy's father had used his personal helicopter to fly them across the country in order to attend the homecoming.

Laughter had been the priority for the day and it was one of her fondest memories. Hurt zinged through her to realize that Micah couldn't claim that memory. He couldn't put the memories together to make sense.

Okay, change of plans. First, she'd go inside and call Cassidy immediately while she had a signal on her phone, then she'd find Micah first thing in the morning and fill him in.

She grimaced. *That's a good plan. Right, God?*

Micah pulled under the overhang in front of the orphanage. "I'll move this later. No sense in leaving it out for someone to steal." Vehicles were a coveted item out here and had to be kept locked up.

"Fine." It was late and Amy was exhausted. Not only from her ordeal, but the tension between her and Micah. If she delayed talking to him much longer, she'd develop an ulcer. She'd try to reach Cassidy one more time, but if that attempt failed, she'd have to tell Micah everything. Including the facts about her mother.

Lightning flashed, thunder rolled and Amy groaned. Time for another storm. She could smell the rain getting ready to fall from the big clouds she knew were overhead. Micah said, "Go on in. We'll talk later."

Nodding, she pulled herself from the jeep, only to feel Micah's hand on her arm. Electric currents flowed from his hand to her heart. She settled back into the seat and looked at him.

He narrowed his eyes, staring into hers as though searching for something. Amy swallowed hard, didn't dare move. Finally, just as she was about to pull away, he said, "I . . . I'm not sure what happened tonight. And I know we'll talk tomorrow. But, I'm . . ." Amy shivered hard, still focused on the feel of his warm hand against her skin.

He blew out a breath. "I guess what I'm trying to say is that I'm enjoying getting to know you and . . . I'm not ready to say goodbye yet, especially not permanently. So, if you have any more dangerous rendezvous planned, could you let me in on them?" He looked at her, not pushing, patient, yet tense, obviously wondering what she would think of his admission.

Amy leaned over, pressed a kiss against his cheek and breathed in the smell of sweat and aftershave. Even battered, bruised and with amnesia, he exuded a strength. At that moment, she was incredibly attracted to him. She'd been in trouble and he'd arrived to rescue her. *Thank You, God.* "I care about you, too, Juan. And I'm eternally grateful that you showed up when you did. I was going to explain . . . but, no, you're right. We'll talk in the morning, okay? Come find me."

"Sure."

Scrambling from the car before she gave in to her emotions and said something she'd regret, she headed for the double doors that led into the main building. Anna met her in the lobby to wrap her in a bear hug, "Are you all right? I know you said you were fine, but . . . are you?"

"I'm all right. Let's go into your office. I need to make two more phone calls."

The two walked the short distance down the hall to Anna's office. Anna shut the door while Amy pulled out her satellite phone. She dialed the police, got the chief and reported a watered-down version of what happened in the alley with Roberto. She left Micah out of it. The chief laughed at her while promising to "look into it." Amy snapped the phone shut, her mind already on the next call she'd have to make — and dreading it. "I really don't want to do this. He's going to hate me."

Anna sighed. "Maybe not. You're building a relationship with him. Letting him see that you're not your mother. And besides, you have to do it."

"I know. You're right. This isn't about me. It's about Micah and reuniting him with the family that loves him. I'll just have to deal with whatever feelings he has for me later. Will you pray with me?"

Anna took Amy's hand. "Absolutely."

A sweet, short prayer later, Amy was ready. She clutched the phone, looked at it. The signal was strong, the battery at full charge. No excuses.

With a deep breath and a firm nod, she punched in Cassidy's number. On the third ring, Cassidy answered. "Hello, Amy, is that you?"

"Cassidy! I'm so glad you answered. I've been trying to get hold of you for days."

"We've been at sea and there weren't any cell towers around. Plus, I haven't even bothered to turn my phone on. There's some tropical storm stirring everything up around here. We're going to be docked for a while. Why? What's wrong? Are you okay?"

Amy ignored the question. "Is Gabe with you?"

"Yes, he's right here. Why? You're starting to scare me."

"Sorry, I just have some . . . news . . . about Micah."

"Micah?" Amy heard the shock in Cassidy's voice. Should she tell her?

"Put your phone on speaker so Gabe can hear, too."

A clicking sound came through the line, then Cassidy's voice came back, although she sounded a little farther away, "Okay, now spill it."

Should she just say it? Or dance around it and then ease on into it?

"Micah's alive," she blurted.

Twin, sharp indrawn breaths echoed in her ear. Amy bit her lip and glanced at Anna. The woman's concerned expression touched her.

"He's what?" Cassidy screeched. "What do you mean? How do you know?"

"He's here at the orphanage."

"Why hasn't he called? Gotten in touch? Where's he been for the last two and a half years? Tell me everything," Cassidy demanded.

Cassidy's voice held a hint of tears, and Amy had to swallow hard to get the next words past the lump in her own throat. "He's here, but he's got amnesia. He doesn't remember anything . . . and I haven't told him yet."

"Amnesia?" Cassidy whispered. "Oh, no. Poor Micah."

"He's going by the name of Juan. Micah was in a coma for eleven months, Cass. But he's doing really well, physically. He just can't get his brain to work right, and there's no medical reason for it. There's a doctor here who practically raised him from the dead." Amy swallowed hard. "Lucas, the doctor, thinks it's probably emotional trauma causing him to block everything out. Then some other things happened —" she'd save those details for later "— and Lucas asked me to postpone telling him. But now I think it's time."

Cassidy wept, and Gabe's voice came on the line. "Amy, you have to tell him who he is."

Amy sniffed back her own tears. "I know. I was going to do that in the morning. Actually, I was going to do that today, but we got involved in a, um, an unexpected . . . adventure and I haven't had the chance."

"We're going to cut our cruise short and fly out there. Maybe seeing all of us will jar his memory." Excitement colored Gabe's voice now that he was getting over the shock of finding out his best friend and fellow SEAL was alive.

"I'm still going to talk to him in the morning. I've got to tell him, although, to be honest, I'm afraid of what he'll say when he remembers that it was my mother that . . ."

Gabe said, "Micah won't hold that against you."

Amy wasn't so sure of that.

"We'll call you when we finalize the details. I'm not sure what's going on with this storm, so we may be stuck here for a while. We're in Nassau, the Bahamas, and they're calling for a hurricane."

"Okay. I'll go break the news to Micah. Pray for him . . . and me."

"We'll be praying, Amy. Bye now."

"Bye," she whispered and hung up.

"Well, that went well." Anna's voice startled her. She'd been so deep in thought she'd forgotten the other woman was still there.

"Pretty well," she muttered. "Let's just

hope the same can be said after my meeting with Micah in the morning."

Morning arrived in a blaze of glory and Juan decided to get to work on the wing while the sun was shining. Thoughts of last night crowded his mind, and he decided the physical labor would be cathartic even though it might be painful. He headed for the tool storage to grab a belt. Jonathas was already there, along with Salvador.

"Bom dia, senhor." Salvador greeted him with a solemn face.

"Good morning, Sal. How are you?"

The boy shrugged and Jonathas stepped up to grab the last belt from the shelf. "He is being a pain today. I don't know what his problem is, but I'm ready to work."

Juan shot the teen a warning look and Jonathas muttered, "Sorry."

Juan patted Salvador on the shoulder and stepped into the wing under construction. A new shipment of lumber gleamed in the morning light. Stacked almost eight-feet tall and loosely roped together, the lumber would be enough to finish the project. He pounded the first nail into the wood, wincing from the pain of his rib. Okay, he thought, sitting back. Maybe he wouldn't be pounding nails. He inhaled the scent of

133

construction mingled with the smell of breakfast coming from the cafeteria. He'd stop by there in about an hour.

Swinging the hammer brought satisfaction, but too much pain. He couldn't do it. He'd have to supervise or something. Eventually, the other workers arrived one by one, coming from various parts of the jungle or the city of Tefe. Everyone exchanged greetings and got to work, not wanting to miss out on an ounce of daylight and the co-operative weather. The forecast called for another thunderstorm later in the day, and Juan wanted to have the walls finished by then. Piece by piece, the plywood went up. As he made the rounds, checking nails, the progress of the other workers and pausing to let his rib rest, he thought about Amy and her crazy trip into Tefe last night.

What was she thinking going off on her own like that? Who had she gone to meet and why? When he'd asked Anna, she'd been vague, saying that it was up to Amy to tell him. He wondered who her attacker had been and why she didn't want to report him to the authorities. What was she hiding? And what "things" had she been going to tell him last night?

Maybe he should have stopped by the dock this morning instead of coming straight to work on the wing. No, she'd find him as she'd promised when she was done with her quiet time. He pictured her sitting out there on the dock, studying her Bible and talking to God. Or would she find a different place to have her quiet time instead of the spot where he'd almost been run over?

He stopped to take a swig of water from the canteen he'd filled earlier and again wondered if he should go find her. One of the workers stepped past him carrying an armload of insulation. Another carried a piece of drywall. Soon the exterior construction would be finished and then they would start on the inside, painting and decorating. The new wing consisted of eight rooms. One parent room with a private bath and sitting area, six children's dormitories with a bathroom between each and one big playroom. It would be fabulous when it was finished.

Once complete, this orphanage would be the nicest in the country. The kids deserved it. They sure didn't deserve the tragedy in their young lives — watching their families die before their eyes, or being left on the doorstep by parents who couldn't afford to feed them or just didn't want them.

Capping his water, he turned to ask one

of the workers a question about the lumber. When he looked up, he stopped. Amy. Standing in the doorway, watching all the action. Their eyes met and she smiled, a worried half smile.

Uh-oh. Something must be wrong.

Hammering, drilling and men chattering in Portuguese echoed all around him, but faded into the background as Amy started toward him. Then her eyes flew wide, horror filling them. He heard the creaking, felt the rush of wind; something knocked him in the back and he went stumbling sideways. Renewed pain arched through him, his rib screeching at the rough treatment. Time slowed. Wood crashed around him, smashing into the floor. Pieces scattered, one slamming into his leg. He went down. Another piece of wood bounced off his shoulder, falling to swipe his knee.

"Micah!" she screamed. Vaguely he wondered who Micah was. Then another piece of lumber clipped the side of his head, tumbling his world from its axis. Landing on his side, he felt a hand grab his arm and yank him out of the way as the rest of the stacked wooden wall smashed all around him. Lights flashed behind his eyes, a sharp pain streaked through his brain. He felt the warm gush of blood trickle down his right cheek. He raised a hand to the wound and looked up to see Amy kneeling beside him.

"Micah, are you all right?" Her hands cradled his wounded head.

The name echoed around him, through him, all over him. *Micah.* He knew that name. His name. Dazed, he whispered, "What?"

"Are you all right?" she repeated. "Your head. Let me look at it." Suddenly, she was all business, the professional nurse she'd been trained to be. "Salvador, get me the first-aid kit in the tool room. Hurry! *Pressa!*"

Salvador stood as though frozen, staring at the dripping blood. Amy raised her voice a notch. "Salvador, now! *Agora!*"

The teen snapped his attention to Amy, then hurried to grab the first-aid kit. He was back in less than ten seconds, and Amy had a square of sterile padding out and on Micah's head in even less time than that.

Micah's ears buzzed. A thousand bees were swarming in and around his head. Then he realized he was looking into a face he'd seen all his life. He was looking into the eyes of Amy Graham, his sister's best friend and the daughter of Senator and Cecelia Graham. The woman who had known his identity and had kept it from him. He stared at her, disbelief and disappointment, hurt and fury, all battling within him. He searched for the words to ask her why and came up empty. He could only stare into those bewitching blue eyes and wonder what really went on behind them.

He knew. She'd seen it in his eyes as soon as she'd said his name. Amy swallowed hard and concentrated on the gash on his forehead. She didn't think it needed stitches, but it could use a couple of butterfly bandages. One hand holding the gauze, she used the other to rummage through the first-aid kit and came up with some disinfectant and two Band-Aids. She affixed them to his head and sat back, never taking her eyes from his.

Heart pounding, she waited for the explosion.

"Amy?" The hurt and confusion in his voice made her wince.

"Welcome back, Micah," she said softly.

"Why?"

She understood every question he had condensed into that one word. Sucking in a deep breath, she stood and placed a hand on his arm. "I'll explain it to you later. We need to get Lucas to check your head."

Micah waved her off. "I'm fine." He

struggled to his feet jerking away from her touch. He glared at her. "I don't think I can afford any more of your help."

Pain like an arrow through her heart nearly sent her back to her knees. Aware of the many eyes still on them, she started, "Micah . . ."

"Never mind. I need to look at something." He limped over to the fallen wood, looked at the pieces for a moment then leaned over to pick up the end of a length of rope. He pulled the rest of it from under the lumber. By this time, Lucas had arrived, called from the medical mission just a boat ride away.

Amy watched him stride over to Micah. "What kind of trouble are you in now? You know, I . . . Good grief, man, what happened to your head?"

Micah held up the rope. The smooth edge taunted him. "This."

Lucas took the rope and examined it. He raised an eyebrow. "You thinking what I'm thinking?"

"Probably."

Amy walked up, looked at the smooth edge of the rope and gasped. "That was cut!"

Lucas quirked a smile at Micah. "Guess she thinks like us, Juan."

"My name's Micah."

Lucas jerked around. "What?"

Amy whispered, "He remembers everything."

Shock rippled across the doctor's features. He took in the bandaged place on Micah's forehead. "Getting knocked on the head brought it all back?"

"Nope." He glared. "Amy calling my name did the trick."

His bitterness hurt, cut her to the quick.

Lucas's eyes darted back and forth between the two. "Okay, obviously there's something going on that you're not saying. Right now, I'm going to pretend I don't sense the undercurrents. Has anyone contacted the police?"

Amy forced her attention away from Micah. Her heart hurt, and she felt the terrible tug of guilt for not saying something earlier. "No, we're just getting ourselves together. I'll make the call."

Anna laid a hand on her arm and said, "I'll take care of it."

"Thanks."

The two men were deep in conversation. Amy slipped away to her room and shut the door. She fell across the bed to pour her heart out.

Oh, Lord, help me here. Someone just tried

to kill Micah again. Who, God? Why? How do I go about helping him? He remembers, and I'm so glad for him, but God, he's going to remember the e-mail he sent my mother, then he's going to have questions. How do I tell him she's the one that betrayed him and caused him to lose two years of his life? He's so angry with me. And I don't really blame him. Soften his heart, his anger. Keep reaching out to him. Show Yourself to him.

A knock on the door brought her to her feet. She opened it to find Carlita standing there, bunny tucked snuggly under her arm. Amy's heart lifted as she leaned over to say in Portuguese, "Hello, little one. What can I do for you?"

Carlita shifted, looked down the hallway. Amy followed her gaze, but saw nothing. "What is it, Carlita?"

Slowly the little girl pulled her hand from behind her back and held it up to Amy. A piece of paper fluttered in her tight grasp.

"For me?" Amy asked.

Carlita shook it at her and Amy took it. "*Obrigada,* sweetheart."

A little smile crossed the girl's bow-shaped lips, and then she walked toward the room she shared with her brother.

She looked down at the note — and gasped. Slipping back into the room, she shut the door. Curling up on the bed, she read, "You've been looking for me. I will be at the little chapel in the jungle tomorrow at six o'clock in the evening. Come alone. If you bring authorities, you will die."

Another note. Could she believe it? Trust that it really was from the woman she'd been trying to contact? Or was it a trick to get her alone again? What should she do? Amy mulled the problem for over an hour. She finally decided she would ask Anna to be there with her, hiding in the chapel. Anna knew how to use a gun, so if something went wrong, between the two of them, they could handle the situation. She couldn't burden Micah with her problems now that he had so much to process.

Tomorrow, at six, she would meet her maternal grandmother for the first time in her life. She just prayed she'd live through the experience to tell about it.

EIGHT

Micah paced his room and closed his eyes against the mad rush of memories. They swirled and twirled like a hummingbird on speed. After Amy had left, Lucas declared that Micah needed to lie down and sent him to his room like a schoolboy. Micah, still in shock, hadn't fought the order, so now he was alone with his thoughts and he couldn't settle his mind on just one.

Every time he focused on one thought, another one intruded. Finally, he just decided to let the memories come in a stream-of-consciousness flow. His family, sister and best friend and fellow SEAL. He, Micah McKnight, was a Navy SEAL. He'd been on a mission with his SEAL buddies and Gabriel Sinclair when the mission went terribly wrong. He frowned and concentrated hard. What *had* gone wrong?

Gabe had practically twisted his arm to get Micah on that mission. Micah had been working on something else, and Gabe's mission had the potential to blow Micah's current cover. Instead, Manuel Cruz, gunrunner, human trafficker, and all-around really bad guy had found out that he was about to be raided and had blown everything to smithereens — including his own son. Micah's heart ached at that memory, ached to his very soul. He could still feel the child's small hand in his, smell the smoke, feel the searing heat of the fire as it licked around them. Then the last explosion had rocked the mansion and the child's hand had slid from his as Micah's world had spiraled into darkness.

Somehow, he'd crawled out of the inferno and reached the jungle. Pain like nothing he'd known before had ripped through him, threatening him with unconsciousness. He remembered Gabe and Manuel locked in combat; Manuel stabbing Gabe. Then Micah pulled the trigger to end the evil one's life. He'd killed a man. Granted, it had been to save Gabe's life, but the thought that he was responsible for the death of Manuel Cruz hit him hard.

Could the man's family have found him at the orphanage? Were they behind the attempts on his life?

He thought about his family. He'd tried

to call them and had gotten nothing except voice mail. Pulling those numbers from his memory had been sweet. They had kept the same numbers, and he figured it probably didn't have a lot to do with a calling plan. They'd kept them for him. In case he could call. Love swelled inside him. He missed them. No, they weren't the perfect family, but they loved each other. And he couldn't wait to catch up with them, see them, hug them.

And Amy had kept that from him. Why? Why would she do such a horrendous thing? What could she have been thinking?

Was everything about her a sham? He pictured her sitting on the dock reading her Bible. Her unwavering care for him when he'd been sick. Her bravery in going after him in the water. Little Carlita snuggled up on her lap with Amy's chin resting on the dark head. No, it wasn't a sham. But there was something else going on, and he intended to find out exactly what.

Then he remembered the e-mail he'd sent to Senator Graham, Amy's father. He sat down hard on the bed. Juanita Morales aka Cecelia Graham, Amy's mother. While on a separate mission, the one before he'd been hurt, he'd come across a picture of a young girl, Juanita Morales, on the wall of the police station. He'd been shocked at the resemblance between the girl and Cecelia Graham and had impulsively sent an e-mail to the senator, asking him if there was a connection. And heard nothing.

After that, he'd been so busy on his next mission that he hadn't really given it much thought. And then Gabe had called, practically forcing him to join the team for the raid on Manuel Cruz. Then Micah's world had literally exploded.

And then Amy called his name.

Was Juanita Morales really Cecelia Graham? What if the Graham family didn't want that to get out? Would the senator do something so rash as to betray his country to keep his wife's background quiet?

If she was Juanita Morales, the political scandal would be enormous. He could easily picture what would appear in the newspapers and magazines. A young girl who disappeared as a teen, thought to have been sold into prostitution, turning up in the United States married to a senator, using a different name and lying about her background?

Men had killed for less.

And he, Micah, had sent an e-mail to the man with a picture of a suspected prostitute who looked like his wife. Had the senator set Micah up to be killed? Had Amy arrived to finish the job? To protect her mother? Although, if that was the case, why was he still alive? She'd known his identity when she'd fished him out of the water.

One of their first conversations ran through his mind. He'd asked her why she was doing what she was doing and she'd said, "Because of my mother."

What had she really meant by that? What did Cecelia Graham have to do with anything?

A knock on his door brought his racing mind to a screeching halt. "Who is it?"

"It's me. Amy."

Amy. Did he want to talk to her yet? Not really, but he couldn't just ignore her. Plus, he had a lot of questions that only she could answer. He pulled himself from the bed and to the door. Yanking it open, he found Amy standing in the hall, twisting a tissue between her fingers.

She still looked beautiful to him in spite of her tear-swollen red eyes. And that made him mad. He had to quit noticing how good she looked.

"Would you walk with me and talk?"

"I don't know that I'm up to talking, but I've got a few questions I wouldn't mind listening to the answers to."

"That's fair." She hiccupped and stuck the tissue into her back pocket. Micah pulled the door shut behind him and fell into step with her as she headed down the hall. They passed through the lobby and exited the double doors at the end. Bright sunlight made him wish he'd brought his sunglasses as he headed for the path that led to the river.

Amy took a deep breath and said, "I'm sorry."

"Just tell me why." He didn't look at her, couldn't. He'd been halfway in love with this woman and now . . .

"A lot of reasons. Albeit most of them would probably be considered selfish."

"Does it have anything to do with your mother?"

She dragged in a ragged breath. "Yes."

It had everything to do with her mother. But what did she say? "It's . . . hard to explain. I don't know if I can find the words."

"You knew who I was and you never even hinted. I need you to find the words." His voice was tense, as though he were controlling his anger with great effort.

Oh, God, please give me the words to say. "I called your parents the minute I figured out who you were. And I haven't known for long. You look so different and we hadn't seen each other for years. You looked familiar, but I didn't really think about it. Micah McKnight was dead. And I didn't know who you were until that day in the jungle when we were hurrying down the path and your shirt ripped. I saw the birthmark and knew."

Surprise flickered. "You called my family?"

She nodded. "I didn't get anything but voice mails for a while because they're on a month-long cruise. Then I finally got in touch with Cassidy and told her you were here."

"So they know I'm safe?"

"Well, they know you're alive. After all that's happened, I'm not sure I'd say you were exactly *safe*." Or safe to be around. Her heart still went crazy around him, even though he still didn't know everything. "But, yes, they know you're alive and that you've had amnesia. They're trying to get here to see you, but that hurricane off the coast of Florida has them grounded right now. They're not sure when their cruise ship will be permitted to sail again."

"That makes me feel somewhat better, but why didn't you tell me as soon as you realized who I was? You knew the agony I was going through, trying to remember," he accused.

Amy hung her head for a moment. "Micah, I'm not the same girl you remember from back home. Growing up for us was one big party. We've always had the easy life, taken the easy road. Yes, I was lonely as a child sometimes, but having you and Cassidy filled that void. My parents were always busy with their politics — and keeping my antics out of the gossip column. I took for granted that nothing would change, I could just skip through life untouched by tragedy. And I certainly didn't need God. But now —" she sucked in a deep breath "— life has been . . . cruel the last few months. My world has been shaken, rocked to the core. And . . ." Oh, how could she put this? She scrambled for words. "I'm trying to make sense out of a lot of things. Especially God, and what He has in mind for me."

He gave a sound of frustration. "What does that have to do with your not telling me who I am?"

She huffed in exasperation. "Nothing. Everything." She threw her hands into the air. "I'm trying to find the words to explain, so you'll understand why I didn't just blurt out that I knew you. Micah, I didn't know if I would do more harm telling you or not. At first, I hesitated for medical reasons because I didn't know what kind of effect telling you would have. A lot of doctors feel like an amnesiac needs to remember at his or her own pace."

Amy stalled. How could she tell him it was her mother that set him up on that mission? Would he think she had anything to do with it?

Another thought struck her. She'd wanted him to get to know her as she was now. Not remember her as she'd been growing up. She reeled with the realization. Where had that come from?

"You said, 'at first.' That means you changed your mind."

Blinking, she focused on what he was saying and responded, "Oh. Lucas overheard a conversation between Anna and me. He told me it would be all right to tell you. So, I said I would. I originally planned to tell you that day of the picnic, but then the dunking booth exploded and you were hurt. Lucas told me not to say anything until you felt better. Later, I went into town and you ended up rescuing me. Then today . . ."

"It was too late."

"Yeah." She sighed.

"Hey, Juan, Amy."

They turned at the call. Relief at the interruption flowed through her. She could hear Micah's molars grinding, but he put a smile on his face and said, "Hello, Chief."

David Ruibero glanced between the two and asked, "Am I interrupting something? You looked as if you were having a pretty serious discussion."

Micah said, "We were, but nothing that can't wait. I've regained my memory and the name's Micah. What can we do for you?"

The man stuck his hands into the back pockets of his pants and looked Micah in the eye. "You remember, that's great. Maybe now you can tell me why someone is trying to kill you."

Micah blinked. "What do you mean?"

"As you suspected, the steering wheel and the gas pedal were jammed. That jeep running you off the dock was no accident. We took fingerprints, but don't know how long it'll take to get anything back. And I don't know that it'll do any good anyway. Probably every staff member at the orphanage has driven that jeep, plus all the kids that have ridden in it at some point. Darts don't come with poison. And homemade but deadly bombs don't just magically appear under dunking booths. Someone is going to a lot of trouble to get rid of you. I'm trying to find out, but not having a whole lot of luck."

Nodding, Micah said, "Well, I appreciate the effort. And to answer your question, I don't have a clue who wants me dead. That's one of the things Amy and I've been trying to figure out."

"What's *he* doing back?"

The surly question caught their attention, and Amy turned to see Jonathas standing in the middle of the path ahead glaring at David. Trying to have a private conversation around here was impossible.

"You want me to lock you up, kid?" Steel underscored the soft-spoken words.

Laughing, Jonathas didn't look the least bit concerned. Amy frowned at the teen's obvious disrespect. "Jonathas, that's enough. David is here to help."

"His kind don't help. They just throw you out on the street and make you beg. Or take money from the rich people who don't want to go to jail, but deserve to."

It was Micah's turn to frown. He glanced at Amy, then David, then back at Jonathas. "I'm not sure what kind of experience you've had with law enforcement, but David here has done nothing but try to help. You might want to be a little more respectful."

The teen's glare bounced from one adult to another. He snorted. "You're all alike." He stomped off before anyone could offer a rebuttal.

Amy sighed and said, "Obviously he's got some issues with the law."

"*Sim,* I'm going to look him up when I get back to the office," David muttered.

"Jonathas is a good kid. He just needs some guidance. And a positive male influence," Amy insisted. Micah grunted, but didn't argue.

"Okay, so where does all this leave us?" she asked.

"What do you mean?" David asked.

"I mean, what's next? Someone tries to smother Micah with a pillow, attempts to shoot him full of holes with poison darts, tries to run him over or hope he drowns attempting to get away from the runaway jeep, blows up the dunking booth and now knocks over those boards. All of those incidents could have had serious consequences. It's just by the grace of God that he's even standing here."

Micah thought about that last statement. She was right. He should be dead several times over by now. Was it really God's grace or just dumb luck? He realized he wanted to believe it was God. Since Amy had arrived, their talks had made God more real to him than He'd ever been before. As a child, Micah had never had much use for God. As a teen, he'd gone to church with a buddy from high school and learned about Jesus dying on the cross for his sins.

During a summer church camp, the band had been the biggest spiritual influence. The lead singer really seemed to get into the whole worship thing, and the speaker had been real, not some put-on job who thought he was above the kids he was preaching to.

Like it was yesterday, Micah remembered when the session was over, the speaker had joined the kids in the dining hall and just hung out. The band, too. It had been one of the coolest experiences in his life. God had seemed so real to him that week, so Micah had gone forward for the invitation and accepted Christ. Then that summer ended and his life had not exactly gone back to *normal,* but he'd definitely put God on the back burner.

When he'd joined the Navy, his spiritual attitude had been to say a quick prayer when he was in trouble and remember to thank God every once in a while when he was safe. Now he realized God was very real. It also hit him that he didn't consider it dumb luck he was still alive. God had spared him from death, was allowing him to get his life right. He swallowed hard, realizing he needed to have a serious talk with God. But right now, he had to focus on what the chief was saying.

"We're still investigating. Anna said that those who set up the dunking booth did so almost first thing in the morning, so almost anyone would have had time to slip those little bombs underneath with no trouble. Meaning, even if we knew exactly who set the booth up, it doesn't mean one of them is our would-be killer."

Micah sighed. "Of course."

"I'll get back to you when I have something. Otherwise, keep your eyes and ears open. No telling what our perpetrator has planned next."

"Will do."

"Ah, Chief," Amy said, "did you find anything out about Roberto?"

The man smirked. "Nothing. I really don't think he was the man you saw in the alley."

Amy disagreed, but kept her mouth shut. She'd done the right thing and told what she'd experienced. As expected, no one believed her. Which suited her purpose right now. She wasn't ready for anyone to raid that camp. Not until she met with her grandmother to see if she had any other relatives here in Brazil.

The chief left. Micah turned his attention back to Amy. Maybe now they could finish their conversation, but Amy's focus was elsewhere.

Salvador came down the path swinging a stick, knocking on the trees. Micah noticed the young man's sullen expression. "Hey, Sal, what's wrong?"

Amy sidled away. "I'll catch up with you later. Why don't you figure out what's going on with Salvador? I promised to help on the wing a little more."

"We're not done, you know."

She dropped her gaze. "I know, Micah. Just give me some time and I'll tell you anything you want to know, okay?"

He let her go. Right now, he'd see what was wrong with Salvador. Later he'd find out what Amy was hiding. Intending to offer his assistance, Micah walked over to Salvador.

The boy glanced up. "What do you care?"

"I care. You want to talk about it?"

Salvador cut his eyes at Micah as though considering the question. "My whole family is gone except Carlita."

Yeah, that would depress just about anyone. Instead of voicing that thought, Micah said, "What do you want to do, Salvador? You're twenty years old with a little sister to take care of. Have you talked to the counselor here?"

The young man snorted. "He's an idiot."

Remembering his own transition from teen to early twenties, Micah could relate to Salvador's thinking that almost all adults were ignorant. Except for those he'd met that summer he'd accepted Christ. But that wasn't going to help Sal now. Or could it? Could he, Micah, talk about a God he still had a lot of questions for? "Have you asked God to help you?"

"Every day. I ask Him what I should do. How can I help Carlita? How can I find Natalia? But I don't get an answer. He is a very quiet God right now. But I am very angry with Him also."

"I guess I can understand that." Micah decided he had his own issues to take up with God in the near future. "What about Carlita? Does she talk to you at all?"

Bony shoulders slumped. "No. Nothing. I will take her to America one day. Then she will be fine."

"What did you see that day? The day the men came and took your older sister away and killed your parents?"

Shudders racked Salvador's thin body as

he fought the memories and looked up at Micah with a glare. Through gritted teeth, he swore, "Nothing. I saw nothing."

Micah hesitated to push the issue. He was no counselor, but even he could see that Salvador's bottling everything up inside wasn't good. "You need to talk about it, Sal."

"I can't," he whispered, agony etched on his young features.

"Think about it, *sim?*"

"Sim." Abruptly, Salvador asked, "You like the woman, don't you?"

"Huh?" Micah blinked, trying to line his thoughts up with Salvador's question.

"Miss Amy. You have feelings for her, don't you? I can tell by the way you look at her."

"Uh, yes, I mean, she seems like a good woman. She cares a lot for you and Carlita."

"Yes, Carlita likes her a lot."

Micah thought he knew where this was going. "Are you afraid Carlita will get attached to Amy and then Amy will leave?"

Salvador shrugged, not offering an answer. He walked off, shoulders still slumped. Micah blew out a breath. Poor kid. Turning his thoughts to his "to do" list, he decided he'd better call the Navy to let them know that he was still alive. Then he'd find out what Amy was up to.

At five-thirty that evening, Amy grabbed a flashlight and a raincoat, slipped into her waterproof boots and opened the door. The hall was quiet, everyone else was in the cafeteria eating the evening meal. She'd grabbed an apple and a tortilla thirty minutes ago. The note said six o'clock. Anna was already there up in the balcony so she could watch to see who came in.

Micah would be in the dining room with the rest of the group. Hopefully no one would be looking for her until later, when she'd promised Carlita she'd be there to tuck her in.

Locking the door behind her, she hurried out into the downpour. Rain, rain and more rain. *Please, God, keep me safe.*

The wind knocked the trees around, the water sluicing down the canopy leaves to splatter on the ground. Amy splashed her way down the path to the chapel at the end. A larger church was attached to the main building, but the little stone chapel had been there for ages. Built in the 1800s, it had once been the center of the village built around it. The village had eventually disappeared, but the chapel still stood.

Amy had discovered it the day after she'd arrived in Tefe. Desperately needing a reprieve from the illness and misery, she'd taken a walk up the path. Upon entering the little door at the back, she'd been pleasantly surprised at how well kept it was. Later she'd learned they had services every Sunday morning out here.

Anna told her that the orphanage had purchased that land and the chapel from the government who'd taken it over when the villagers dispersed.

Now Amy told her stomach to settle down while she worked to control her erratic breathing. Nerves, fear and doubt shuddered through her. *For God did not give us a spirit of fear, but of power and of love and of a sound mind.* II Timothy 1:7 ran through her mind as she placed her hand on the doorknob. She was sure Micah would question the "sound mind" part if he knew what she was getting ready to do. She wished she could ask for his help in this venture, but didn't think he would agree. He was too angry right now. No, this was the best way. The only way. And Anna would be waiting inside for her. Anna would hide and call for help if needed. But she honestly didn't think she'd need any help. Not this time.

Right, Lord?

Taking a deep breath didn't help, so she opened the door and walked in, standing still to give the water time to pool at her feet. Musty air greeted her in spite of the chapel having been used this past Sunday. But it wasn't the mustiness of dirt, it was the smell of ancient days, rich in history. She loved this place, wished she was there under different circumstances. But right now she needed to hurry. A glance at her watch told her time was passing quickly.

To her left, a winding staircase led up to the balcony. She wondered if she should chance being trapped up there. What if Maria brought someone with her? What if Amy was putting her trust completely in the wrong person? Not that she really trusted Maria, but . . . She sighed and shivered. It was chilly in here, well insulated against the heat of the tropics.

Anna, hiding in the balcony, gave Amy a small wave. Amy waved back then looked around, deciding she needed a place that would allow her to observe whoever entered, yet would have easy access for escape should she need it.

The baptism pool.

She hurried to the front of the chapel, passed the stained-glass windows depicting the crucifixion and up the two steps that led to the pool. Not a traditional baptismal, it was more like a miniature pond surrounded by stones and natural jungle vegetation. The wooden floor had been built around a small tree. Anna explained that the tree had to be cut every so often to keep it from reaching the roof.

A scrape sounded at the door.

Amy's heart nearly leaped from her throat. She needed to hide. Now.

She scurried around the tree, praying the door behind the pool wasn't locked. She didn't have time to try it. Maria had arrived early, too.

Micah stared at the short stocky woman as she turned the knob to enter the small chapel. Who was she? Why was she meeting Amy here? Actually, Micah thought, the woman looked very familiar, yet he couldn't place her. She didn't work at the orphanage, that he was sure of. Maybe someone from the hospital. A nurse?

He shook his head. No. It was the police station. Her picture was on the wall. Disbelief sucked the air from his lungs as he realized Amy was meeting with a wanted felon.

Following her had been a spur-of-the-moment decision. He'd seen her walk by the cafeteria and out the door dressed for the rain. Curious, he'd stepped out to ask her where she was going, but she'd been focused . . . driven, secretive. So he'd kept his mouth shut and skulked after her.

And now he just discovered her meeting with a known rebel, a woman who sheltered killers and human traffickers. Sorrow shook him. Surely she wasn't involved with these people. Micah thought about everyone at the orphanage who'd accepted him, fed him, cared for him. Lucas, who practically brought him back to life.

Anger took over. He felt like a fool. He'd trusted her, believed in her and her faith. *Have I been a fool, God? Has she completely tricked me in to believing everything she said? How can she do this?*

If Amy put any of those wonderful people in danger with whatever she was into, he'd see to it she paid. And paid dearly. In the meantime, he'd give the two of them a little time to get comfortable, then he'd make his presence known.

The door opened and the covered figure entered the back of the chapel. Peering around the tree, Amy watched as the woman pulled back her hood.

Maria Morales. No mistaking that face.

The woman looked around, but didn't seem to be interested in hiding. In fact, after about a minute, she slid into the very back pew and bowed her head as though praying. Stunned, Amy could only wonder at Maria's actions.

Slowly, Amy eased from behind the tree. The wooden floor creaked and Maria's head shot up.

"It's me. Amy."

Expressionless, the woman said, "You are smart. You arrived early, too."

Amy shrugged, "I'm meeting a woman whose face is on a wanted poster in the police station. I'm not sure I'd call that smart."

A hint of a smile almost crossed Maria's lips. Amy wondered if that was a figment of her imagination. Maria said, "You are trying to find me. I am here. What do you want?"

For a moment, words escaped her and Amy just stood and stared at the woman. Finally she blurted, "You're my grandmother."

Still no expression. "So I heard."

Amy sidled closer. "You have contacts in the police department. The man who attacked me warned me away from you."

"Yes, he warned me also."

"Really?"

"Warned me to have no contact with you. The woman claiming to be my grand-daughter."

"My mother is Juanita Morales."

"Juanita. Then she is alive?" A slight catch in her voice clued Amy in. The woman wasn't completely unfeeling. And her eyes said she had accepted Amy's claim as true.

"She's alive." She left it at that. No sense in revealing Juanita's current address was the county jail. Not until Amy had some kind of hint that Maria was going to help her find any remaining relatives she might have left in this country.

"Do you know anything of your uncle? Rafael?" The question seemed forced, as though Maria was loath to ask it.

Maria didn't know? Amy twitched, wondering whether she should tell her Rafael had been murdered in jail after he'd been arrested for trying to kill Cassidy. She settled for simply saying, "He . . . died."

A deep breath was the only indication of the woman's distress. "I see."

Amy rushed on. "I'm a friend of Cassidy McKnight. Do you remember her? She was in your camp, kidnapped from this orphan-age."

"*Sim,* I remember her. What about her?"

"She said you kept her safe from Rafael."

"This is also true. He had no business messing with her. I knew her family would not give up looking for her. If Rafael harmed her, he would only bring trouble down onto the camp."

Ignoring that explanation for a moment, Amy got to the part she was really interested in. "Do I have any other relatives?"

Maria tilted her head and narrowed her eyes, studying Amy as though trying to read her. Finally, she nodded once, then said, "Yes, one. You have a cousin who lives in the camp. She is twelve."

"A cousin," she breathed, stunned yet thrilled. "Twelve years old. Is she happy?"

"I don't know. I never asked her. She does what all girls in the camp do. She works hard and keeps her mouth shut."

Inwardly, Amy shuddered at the picture of such a dreadful life. Then a thought came to her. Maybe, she could make a difference in her cousin's life and make up for some of the destruction her mother had wrought. "Would she be willing to come to America with me if I could arrange it?" she asked.

"Why?"

Stepping closer, Amy held out a beseeching hand. "Because we need to get her away from there. Do you really want her growing up and living that kind of life? Wondering every day if she's going to live or die? Sold into prostitution?"

Anger snapped in the black eyes. "She is twelve years old. Do you really think I would allow that to happen?"

"Do you really think you can you prevent it?" Amy whispered.

This statement finally evoked some emotion on the blank face, some agitation evident in her body language. Maria stood, paced to the door and back. "This is not the life I would have chosen for my children — or my grandchildren. But it was the life of my husband. If I tried to resist him, he'd beat me." A shrug followed a weary sigh. "Your cousin, her name is Lucia. Do you really think you can help her? What do you plan to do with her?"

"Take her back to the United States. Give her a chance at a normal life. I just don't know what it'll take or how to go about it legally."

Maria let out a long slow exhale, rolling her shoulders as though trying to throw off the tension. Flatly, she said, "She is an American citizen."

Now that was unexpected. "What? How?"

"Brigitte, Lucia's mother, was an American. I do not know how she and Rafael met.

168

All I know is that Rafael was gone for a long time and when he returned, he had his wife and newborn baby with him. One month after they arrived, Brigitte died in a car bombing in Rio de Janeiro. Organized crime is rising and the police can do nothing." She shrugged. "The rebels hide in the forest where no one can find us."

"I found you."

A wry chuckle took Amy aback. Maria declared, "No, I found you."

"Okay," she drew the word out slowly. "I guess that's true. All that aside, will you help me get her out of this life? Will you try to get out yourself? You can come back to the United States, live with me."

Maria shook her head slowly. "No, not me. I am here until I die, but Lucia . . ." She briefly closed her eyes. When she opened them, they were softer, almost wistful. "I will think on what you have said. I will contact you within a week. Do not look for me before that. I am not the only one that knows you are here. Many in the camp do because of our contact in the city."

"The policeman, Roberto."

Narrowing her eyes, she said, "Yes. Do not go anywhere alone. If he knows that you saw his face that night, he will come after you. He is very angry with the one you call

Juan. Roberto is even meaner than Rafael. He wears the uniform of the good side, but you do not want to see his bad side. Unfortunately, if he can get you alone, he will probably kill you and the other man. The one who beat him in the alley."

Amy shuddered. "I've already seen his bad side, and you're right, I have no desire to see it again. We'll be careful. And God will look after us."

Maria stood. "I don't know about your God —" she crossed herself "— but if you are talking about the God Christians believe in, then I pity you. He has shown His weakness. He has no power. All I see in this world is evil. I hope you do not become one of its many victims."

Amy wanted to weep at this statement. How could she reach the woman? Would she have the opportunity to share Christ with her?

Twenty feet away, the door started to swing open. With a finger to her lips, a warning in her eyes, Maria headed to the front of the chapel where the second exit was. She slipped out the front at the same time Micah slipped in the back.

Amy stared at him. What was he doing here?

NINE

"What are you doing here, Amy?" Micah took no pleasure in her surprise at his presence; he just wanted to figure out what was going on.

"No, Micah, that's my question? What are *you* doing here?"

Shutting the door on the rain that still pounded, he stepped into the lobby. A quick shake of his dark head flung water droplets everywhere. "Following you," he answered.

Outrage flickered across her face. "What gives you the right?"

"The same thing that gave you the right to keep my identity a secret."

She flinched. Micah winced. Okay, maybe that had been a shot below the belt.

He looked around and asked, "You want to tell me what you're doing consorting with a known criminal?"

"None of your business."

Fury exploded through him. "I'm making

it my business! In case you haven't noticed, someone's tried to kill me several times over the last few days. Call me paranoid, but your actions don't add up. You don't tell me my identity, you're obviously hiding something and now you're having a rendezvous with a woman who's on a wanted poster. What am I supposed to think?"

"You're not supposed to think anything. I came here for answers to my own questions. I may need to find those answers before I can do anything about yours."

Muscles tensed in reaction to his almost overwhelming desire to hit something. Forcing himself to relax, he took in a calming breath. "Look, we still need to talk. I should be on the phone with the cops and have them out here combing the grounds looking for that woman."

"No, don't do that!"

In agitation, Micah scraped a hand down the side of his face that bore his scars. "No, I don't suppose there's any point now, is there? We both know how fast the justice system moves out here — when it moves at all, that is." He paced forward, back. "Is there somewhere we can go to finish our discussion from earlier in the day?"

"I need to tuck Carlita into bed. I promised."

Micah didn't know what to think. She was apparently on friendly terms with a murderer and yet she was worried about breaking a promise to a six-year-old who wasn't even her own child. He felt like throwing up his hands and letting out a massive yell.

Instead he looked at his watch. Seven forty-five. "Meet me in the kitchen at eight-thirty. If you don't show up, I'll hunt you down."

Oops, that was the wrong tone to take and wrong thing to say. Amy narrowed her eyes, stepped forward and jabbed a finger in his chest. "Don't threaten me, Micah."

"Or what?"

"I don't know what," she blustered, "but you'll be sorry."

"I already am sorry," he murmured.

She flinched and turned to go. He grabbed her arm, pulled her back. "I'm not finished. I mean, I'm sorry you feel you can't trust me. I'm sorry you're so bullheaded that you refuse to ask for help. I'm not your enemy, Amy. We've known each other forever. You've been a little sister to me since you kicked me in the shins for locking Cassidy in the closet because she was getting on my nerves. Why is it so hard for you to trust me?"

"I know you're not the enemy."

"Then let me in on what's going on."

"I can't!" Raw emotion ripped from her throat. He blinked. She really thought she couldn't tell him. But why? She stomped away, came back. "You're right. We've known each other forever, Micah. You're black and white, right or wrong. In your eyes, the end does *not* justify the means. You see everything as one choice or the other. And maybe that's the way it should be." She gave a weary shrug. "Right now, I'm not sure what I think. I just know that I'm trying to offer my help to . . . someone and I can't have the authorities in the way until it's done."

"Well, that's clear as mud."

"I know." She reached up and cupped his rough cheek. "I'm sorry. I want to tell you and I will, but could you just give me a little time?"

Micah felt the touch of her hand all the way to the depths of his heart. Her eyes begged him to understand, to keep his questions to himself for the time being. He brought his hand up and covered the one she still had on his cheek. "For now. But just promise me you won't do anything else that has *stupid* written all over it."

She gave a teary chuckle. "The only promise I can make is to promise to try.

Now, let me go tuck in a little girl."

Micah watched her walk off, scanned the perimeter of the chapel and saw no one. However, he couldn't shake the feeling that someone had been watching from the shadows.

Amy was sure Anna had snuck out of the chapel after she and Micah had vacated it and could only hope the woman hadn't been too embarrassed by the scene. Truthfully, Amy had been so absorbed in everything, she'd forgotten poor Anna up in the balcony. She'd apologize later. Right now, she hurried to Carlita and Salvador's room.

A quick glance at her watch showed 8:00 p.m. Bedtime for the little ones. Salvador would probably be in the television room. This morning, Carlita had run up and grabbed Amy around the waist, clinging, crying, yet still not making a sound.

Her heart breaking for the little girl, Amy had held her for an hour, rocking, singing, soothing. Anything to make the child feel better. Carlita had finally slid from her lap and run off to play, but the anguish contained in that small body clenched itself around Amy's heart and squeezed until it hurt to breathe.

Lightly, she knocked on the door to the

room. Before she could step in, Anna came out of her office and headed down the hall toward Amy.

"Is everything all right?" she asked.

"As right as it can be, I suppose. I'm just here to tuck the little one into bed."

"How's Micah? I tried not to listen in, but . . ."

Amy closed her eyes briefly. "It's not your fault. I appreciate your willingness to be there to back me up — and I apologize for the scene. As for Micah, he's . . . not so fine. Understandably so. But I just can't tell him everything yet. Now that I've found out about Lucia, I want to make sure I can get her away from here if Maria decides to let her go. Knowing Micah, he'd insist on getting involved and the man's in enough danger as it is from someone unknown. No sense in giving someone else another reason to hurt him."

"I don't know that I totally agree with what you're doing. If Maria does help Lucia leave, they'll both be considered traitors. You're right. You need to start preparing to get her out."

Amy threw her hands up. "Should I do something differently? If I tell the authorities about Maria and the camp — I don't know the location, but they might have an idea of where it is — they would go in there with guns blazing. And that's assuming their police informant hasn't let the rebels know in advance to disappear."

Nodding, arms crossed over her chest, Anna said, "You're probably right. This country is so different. So volatile. You try desperately to make a right decision — like letting law enforcement know about dangerous felons hiding out in the jungle — and it's very possible that could be the wrong decision. Especially since you know they have a traitor on the force. You and I, we're Americans. We might move here, fall in love with the people and the place, but we'll never be natives. They have their own customs, their own way of dealing with things. Don't let that get you in trouble, Amy."

The words cut deep into her heart, but she knew what Anna as trying to say. "I'll do my best not to. Thanks for the words of advice."

Anna smiled, leaned over and gave Amy a hug. "Tell Carlita I said, good-night."

"Sure." Amy opened the door and stepped into the room. Carlita lay on the bed, her stuffed bunny tucked up under her chin. She looked up at Amy and smiled a sweet little-girl smile that captured Amy's affections in a way she couldn't describe. The clean scent of a recent bath teased Amy's nose.

Leaning over the bed, Amy placed a kiss on Carlita's downy soft cheek. " 'Night, little one."

Carlita's arms wound around Amy's neck and gave her a gentle squeeze. Tears tried to leak out of Amy's eyes, but she forced them back. *Please, Lord, help this little girl and her brother. Send them a family to love them and teach them about You.*

Out loud, she offered a short prayer in her Portuguese, which was improving daily. After another quick squeeze, she stood up and tucked the covers around the little girl who rested her chin on her ever-present bunny. Amy said good-night one more time as she drew the mosquito netting around the bed.

Carlita gave a contented smile and closed her eyes.

As Amy turned to leave, motion to her right caught her attention. She managed to muffle her scream as she realized who it was. "Salvador," she gasped. "You scared me half to death."

"Sorry, Miss Amy. I was just coming to check on Carlita. I didn't realize you didn't hear me come in."

Catching her breath, Amy placed a hand over her racing heart. "No, it's okay. I guess I'm a little jumpy."

Salvador eyed his now sleeping sister. "She likes you."

"I like her, too."

"I'm going to take her to America one day soon. To get her the help she needs."

"I know you will, Salvador. You have a good night and I'll see you in the morning."

Praying for strength and wisdom, she went to meet Micah.

Micah paced the empty kitchen, alternating between praying and doubting. What was Amy up to? Would she talk to him or shut him out again. If she chose to clam up, how would he react? Could he accept giving her the time she said she needed? And in the meantime, did he trust her? Or should he keep her close in order to keep an eye on her?

The Amy he knew from childhood, and even on into adulthood, had been a self-serving little brat. Not once could he remember her doing anything to help someone else. She and Cassidy had been two of a kind, sneaking out of the house, partying at the local bars with fake IDs, getting into whatever mischief they could find. Fortunately, their shenanigans never landed them in legal troubles, but their antics were enough to cause their parents — and one older brother — a few gray hairs.

Only the Amy he now knew seemed to be an entirely different person. Someone who thought about others first. And she read her Bible daily. The Amy he'd known a few years ago would never have been concerned about someone unless they were too sick to go shopping. And that had to constitute a near-death experience, he recalled.

"I'm here."

Tentative, a little worried, her voice came to him from the kitchen entrance. Steeling himself against the desire to take her in his arms and tell her everything would be okay, he leveled his gaze on her.

"Tell me the truth, Amy. Do you know what happened two and a half years ago? Why that highly confidential mission went wrong and literally blew up in our faces?"

Anguish crossed her features. If she bit her lip any harder, she'd bite right through it. "Yes, I know."

"Tell me."

"My mother is Juanita Morales."

"The woman on the missing-persons poster. I e-mailed it to your father, asking if it was your mother. They looked so much alike, I couldn't believe it. I figured it was just a fluke, but thought I'd see what he had to say about it."

Amy wandered into the room, arms crossed in front of her stomach. "My father never saw that e-mail."

Micah frowned. "Oh, I thought it might have been him who set me up."

A huge sigh escaped Amy's lips. "No, that would have been my mother."

Shock zipped up his spine. "Your mother? I never considered . . ."

Lips tight to control their quivering, she nodded. "My father is on the United States Senate Select Committee on Intelligence. He has access to all of the Special Forces missions information."

"But you just said it was your mother."

Frustration flushed her face. "I know. Just . . . be quiet a minute, will you?"

Micah gritted his teeth, drew in a deep breath and blew it out slowly. She paced in front of him. He let her. Finally, she stopped, scrubbed her eyes with the heel of her palms. When she looked up, she looked straight at him. "Do you know where all of our precious family money came from? Not from some healthy inheritance that I've always believed existed. Oh no, my grand-father, my father's father, died broke."

181

Micah simply listened, not wanting to interrupt now that she was telling him what he wanted to know.

Through fresh tears, she continued, "My mother couldn't stand the thought of becoming some middle-class, working woman. After all, she'd married a senator. So, she contacted the brother she'd sworn never to see again after he'd sold her into prostitution when she was a teenager and basically destroyed her."

Disbelief shuddered through him. That didn't mesh with the picture he had of Cecelia Graham. "Oh, boy."

Amy gave a hard laugh. "Yes, oh, boy, indeed. So, she decided to go into business with her brother, my *uncle*." Micah flinched when she spat the word as though it contained poison. "The two of them ran a profitable human-trafficking ring. Everything was obviously going along nicely until my father and your father were up for the ambassadorial appointment. She honestly thought there was no way my father would lose that appointment. And when he did, she knew what Jonathan McKnight's focus would be."

"Human trafficking. Dad's always said he and the president would go after them if he ever had a chance."

"Mother had made a whole new life for herself. She got out of this country, watched how the rich lived, where they went. She spent years perfecting herself. Then she met my father and figured she'd made it."

"But —" he started. Amy held up a finger, and he snapped his lips shut.

"I'm getting there. So —" she hauled in another deep breath while swiping away a few stray tears "— when your father got the appointment, my mother knew of his love for the people of Brazil and that he abhorred that human trafficking was so prevalent in this country. She was afraid that all the effort he'd put in on eradicating human trafficking would cause her *business* to suffer. She wanted to take his focus from his job . . . and get rid of the only other person who knew her real identity, or at least the person she assumed knew her real identity because of the e-mail . . . you. She intercepted it, hacked into my father's computer and work files and set you up — you and two teams of SEALs — to be wiped out."

Sobs threatened to overtake her. Micah watched her through a fog of anger and disbelief as she struggled to control her emotions. He wanted to feel sorry for her. He wanted to feel . . . nothing. But like clips from a horror movie, all he could feel was the anguish of watching his buddies die and the smell of fire as it consumed the building around him.

It just hit him. The mission. He'd lost friends. Good men had died, wives had buried husbands, children would never know their fathers. . . . all because of this woman's mother — and greed. Because of money. He almost doubled over with nausea. It was all he could do not to fall to his knees.

Sheer effort kept him on his feet. He'd been so focused on finding out what Amy knew, he hadn't allowed himself to remember all that *he* knew — until now. He'd grieve later. Right now, the fury building inside him had to have an outlet. "So, why are you here, Amy? To finish the job your mother started?"

TEN

Amy slid to the floor and wept. She deserved it. Everything he said. His anger, his suspicions, possibly his hate. Telling him was worse than she'd dreamed. Not only was he furious, he was deeply hurt. A soul-deep hurt she wondered if he would ever recover from.

"I'm sorry. I'm so sorry," she whispered.

"Yeah, I am, too." She flinched at the coldness in his voice. *What do I do, Lord? He hates me now. Help me.* Her heart cried out to the God who'd never let her down.

"I don't know what to say to you, Amy." A ragged sigh escaped him. "I don't know what to think. I was out of line with that accusation and for that I'm sorry. And I don't necessarily blame you for your mother's actions, but I don't know that I can get past it, either."

"I should have told you. I wish I'd told you, but I can't change that any more than

I can change what my mother did." She beseeched him, hand out, palm up.

"Mentally, I know that." He paced, up one side of the stainless steel counter, then back down toward her. She watched his restlessness, wishing she had the magic words, but try as she might, she couldn't find them in her overloaded brain. He raked a hand down his face. "I have to go."

"No, wait," she scrambled up, still swiping her endless supply of tears, shoving aside her need to curl up into a ball and weep herself into unconsciousness. "Wait, I need to ask you something."

"You don't think you've said enough?"

Another splintering pain shot through her, but she ignored it. She had to be strong, had to ask him for his help now that she'd torn his world apart.

A knock on the door startled them both. Anna poked her head around and grimaced. "I hate to interrupt, but I've got a sick kid on my hands. I really need one of you to go find Lucas and fast. I can't get him on his satellite phone and I think Maya is having an allergic reaction to something. I've given her an antihistamine, but this qualifies as an emergency."

Amy didn't bother to hide her blotchy face, red eyes and tearstained cheeks from her friend. Anna would get it out of her eventually, anyway. Micah, on the other hand, immediately volunteered to go find Lucas.

No doubt, he was concerned for the little girl, but this was also his way to escape an emotionally charged situation. Amy watched him leave, deciding that it was probably for the best. Maybe after they'd both cooled down, they could try to talk again.

Micah hurried past Anna. Anna then turned to Amy with a raised brow, the questions on her pretty face nearly caused Amy to break down once again. She held up a hand, forestalling anything Anna might say. "I can't talk about it right now."

Compassion softened her friend's face. "Sure. You come tell me when you can. I'm here to listen, you know that."

Tears threatened to overflow once again, but through sheer force of will, Amy managed to keep them from falling. "Thanks," she whispered, and headed to her room.

Maya would be fine and Anna was still waiting to talk. Amy didn't want to talk. Not to Anna anyway.

The next day, Amy went through her tasks mindlessly, performing her duties as best she could, trying to focus, but was constantly distracted with thoughts of Micah. Finally, supper had come and gone. Micah had avoided her all day and Amy decided her best course of action was to let him have his space. Only minutes before he'd passed by her, started to say something, then turned on his heel, his body language practically shouting that his anger still seethed.

Needing something to do, she busied herself in the medical center stocking the shelves, thinking and praying. *Lord, there's nothing more I can do. I've told him everything about my mother . . . now . . . what do I do, God?*

Find him.

Amy placed the package of bandages on the shelf. "I don't want to find him, God. My heart's already in pieces, why give him the opportunity to shred what's left?"

She felt herself being called to find him.

"Are you insisting I do this?"

The command still echoed in her mind.

"Okay," she grumbled, thinking. Where would he go?

The workout room in the gymnasium.

What about his rib? Wouldn't that hurt?

Tossing the rest of the bandages back into the box, she left the room to exit the lobby doors, running down the covered walkway to the gymnasium. Darkness had already fallen and although it was still raining, it seemed to be slacking off. She pulled open the heavy doors and listened.

Thunk, grunt. Thunk, grunt. Yep, he was definitely working out his anger. *Okay, God, I'm here. What now?*

Hurrying down the hall, she decided to ask Micah for help in getting her cousin out of the country. She'd convince him to do something for someone instead of holding his anger in — or taking it out on the weights, or her. Specially trained, his skills would enable a rescue to go much more smoothly than if she tried to do this alone or with hired help.

Besides, she'd promised to tell him when she had any more ideas that had *stupid* written all over them. And this one had *stupid* written in big bold letters. Following the sounds coming from the weight room, she hurried down the hall. Thunder sounded in the distance. She shivered in the eerie stillness.

"Micah?"

No sooner had the word left her mouth than darkness dropped over her like a blanket. She stopped moving, reached out a hand to touch the wall. What happened? Had the storm knocked out the power?

A scrape sounded in front of her, then

running feet. Fear darted through her, causing her to tremble. Fumbling in the pocket of the raincoat she'd worn for her meeting with Maria last night, she gripped the flashlight and pulled it out. Flicking the switch, the beam cast a bright light on the wall. "Micah? Who's there?"

It was awfully quiet. Why wasn't he answering? A sound coming from the weight room caught her ear. Cautiously, she approached trying to identify the noise. Again, she heard it. Something scraped along the floor. She whispered, "Micah, are you all right?"

Still no answer. Should she go forward or go find help? No, she couldn't leave now. What if he was lying there hurt and needed help immediately?

Another sound followed by an indrawn breath reached her straining ears.

Drawing on every ounce of courage she possessed — and some she didn't — Amy turned the corner and swung the beam of light inside. She reached out a hand to flick the light switch.

Nothing.

Waving the flashlight around the room, the beam flickered cross Micah. He lay still on the bench, his arms fully extended above him, quivering, sweat pouring from him like the rain outside. Light from the lamppost outside the window illuminated the room in an eerie glow.

"Micah?" she whispered again. Then noticed his eyes fixed on the bar above him. She raised the light and gasped.

A snake stretched the length of the bar, forked tongue flickering with lazy disdain for the man struggling not to disturb it. She dropped the beam to the floor. Another snake slithered under the bench. Muscles quivering Amy did her best to ignore the instinct that wanted to send her screaming from the room.

Oh, please, Jesus, not snakes.

"Micah, I'm going to get help. I can't help you on my own."

"What do you need help with, *senhorita?*"

Amy froze. Jonathas. Relief nearly wilted her. "S-s-snakes," she stuttered.

Jonathas moved from behind her, his eyes followed the beam of her light and stopped. "Oh, not good." The boy had the gift of understatement.

"This crazy man is lifting weights with a bruised rib," she muttered under her breath. Louder, she said, "We've got to do something fast. Micah can't hold that bar up much longer." In fact, his arms seemed to be quivering a lot more than when she'd first walked in.

Jonathas scanned the room. "The Sucururu snake. Very dangerous. Run. Get a gun."

Without hesitation, Amy handed Jonathas the flashlight and sped from the room, into the dark hall, trailing her fingers along the wall to help guide her out the door and to the next building into the main lobby. Her mind registered the brightly lit room. Why was the power on here and not in the other building? She dashed down the hall to Anna's office, burst in and stopped short. Lucas held Anna, who'd obviously been crying, in a tender hug. Flabbergasted, she gaped, but gasped, "I need a gun."

The two stumbled apart. Lucas cleared his throat. Anna gaped. Amy teared up, desperate. "Please, Micah's in danger. Snakes. I need a gun."

Lucas snapped into action. "Anna, give me the key." She did.

He hurried to the cabinet behind Anna's desk, opened it and pulled out a pistol. Amy grabbed it from his hand, ignored his surprised yell and took off back down the hall toward the gym. *Please, God, please.*

Thundering footfalls followed her, but she never slowed. Less than a minute later, she stood shivering next to Jonathas. Micah looked ready to pass out. The snake on the bar had moved to one end, curled around the weight. Micah struggled to hold it upright, but the snake was large and heavy, pulling the weight down toward his face as he grew weaker. Bobbing and weaving, the snake's head moved right, then left, the tongue flickering, testing the air. Amy shoved the gun into Jonathas's hand and took the flashlight from him, keeping it trained on the reptile. Jonathas raised the revolver, took aim and pulled the trigger. The snake's head disappeared.

She didn't flinch, her concern and attention focused on Micah.

Micah slowly lowered the bar to rest on the Y-shaped arms. A small grunt escaped him, his breath coming in quick pants along with a few short groans. The other snake on the floor curled around one of the bench's legs, close to Micah's right leg. The reptile turned, slithered up over his leg; Amy bit her lip to hold back her cry.

Continuing over the lower part of his leg, the snake moved on, up over his knee. Micah's thigh muscle jumped, quivered. The snake drew back, up, opened its mouth, fangs bared. Amy heard the click of the hammer on an empty chamber. Jonathas muttered, "No."

Before she could think twice, she let the flashlight fly.

Micah's muscles could stand no more. The pain in his side drummed. *Dumb, dumb, dumb.* Who lifts weights with a cracked rib? The feel of the snake creeping over his right leg had him clenching his jaw even tighter. Jonathas couldn't shoot the snake without putting a bullet in his leg. Would it be better to be shot or bitten? Probably shot. Less internal damage.

"Shoot it," he grunted.

Then his thigh muscle gave an involuntary jump, bumping the snake's underbelly. That made the reptile mad. Again, the muscle spasmed. The snake's brown-and-black head rose, the mouth opened, and Micah stared into the fangs, already expecting to feel the bite. Better to let it sink its teeth into his upper thigh, not his hand. Farther away from his heart.

Absently, he heard the click of Jonathas's gun. Then something flew right into the snake's head knocking it sideways off his leg. Micah rolled to the left and landed on the floor with a thump. He had no strength to do anything else. Then the crack of a gun shattered the silence and the snake lay still.

Without moving any muscles except the

ones in his neck and eyes, he glanced toward the door.

Lucas.

Jonathas's shot had failed, but Lucas had nailed the reptile. Micah lowered his head back to the floor, gasping, forcing oxygen into his lungs — and prayed. His rib still throbbed, sending pain shooting through him, up into his shoulder, across his back.

But he was alive. Again. *Thank You, God, one more time.*

He felt a hand on his arm. Forcing his eyes open, he stared into Amy's tear-soaked eyes. She asked, "Are you okay?"

"Yeah. Thanks. This time I'm grateful for your softball days." He shoved himself into a sitting position, barely able to command his Jell-O-like muscles. As he shifted, his gaze scraped across an object under the window. "Look."

Amy followed his gaze. "What is it?"

A brown cloth bag lay underneath the window. The screen that had been replaced after the dart incident had been pulled away. "Somebody let those snakes loose in here."

Anna hovered in the doorway with Jonathas. Lucas walked over and kicked — gently — at the bag with the toe of a boot. "No more snakes. Just those two."

195

"But you weren't planning to be in here," she blurted to Micah. "This isn't your normal workout time. How would this person know . . . ?"

"He's watching me. Waiting for the chance." Micah clenched a fist and smacked it into his open palm. "This guy is really starting to make me mad."

"You didn't hear him? When he opened the window? Took the screen off?" Amy stared at him.

Micah's jaw jumped. "I let my guard down . . . again. I wasn't hearing much of anything when I entered this room. The guy could have sent a marching band through here and I wouldn't have noticed. I only noticed the snake from the bar as it crawled up the side of the bench. I thought it was going for my head, but it kept going up my arm and settled itself on the bar."

Amy shivered. "Who's after you, Micah?"

He glared at her. "I don't know, Amy. Why don't you tell me?"

Placing her hands on her hips, she stamped a foot. "I didn't have anything to do with it and you know it!"

"Hey, what's going on with you two?" Lucas asked.

Dropping his head to his chest, Micah sighed. "Nothing." He looked at Amy.

"Yeah, I know. I'm just . . . Never mind. I'm wondering if somehow the family of the man that I killed two and a half years ago is involved."

"But how would they know where to find you? How would they know you're alive?"

Jonathas laughed, but the sound lacked humor. Everyone stared at him. He shrugged. "It would be easy to find this one. Anyone who goes into town would see his picture on all the flyers posted everywhere. Anyone who knew him could find him."

Lucas sighed. "I'll call the chief."

After the excitement of the night before, Amy awoke late, although she didn't mean to. Surprised she'd slept at all, she squinted at the digital clock. Eight o'clock! Why hadn't her alarm gone off? A closer look revealed she'd forgotten to set it. Breakfast started at seven-thirty.

Tossing back the mosquito netting and the covers, she popped out of bed. Hurrying into the bathroom, she took a quick shower, brushed her teeth and dressed, all in under fifteen minutes.

Finished with her morning routine, she hung the towel on the rack. Movement caught the corner of her eye. Her reflection in the mirror. How long had it been since

197

she'd studied herself? She leaned in, noticing that in spite of the sunscreen she slathered on three times a day, sunburn had turned her nose pink. A dusting of freckles skipped across her cheeks and when she smiled, a few more lines at the corners of her eyes crinkled in response. Those hadn't been there last time she'd checked. Her blue eyes looked sad. She blinked, squinted for a closer look, deciding she'd aged over the past few weeks.

Dealing with Micah hadn't helped. He was constantly in her thoughts. She remembered that he'd always been a special man. His parents' wealth hadn't fazed him. Yes, he'd enjoyed the benefit of it, but it hadn't spoiled him like it had Cassidy. And while Cassidy had gotten past that, it hadn't been easy for her. For Micah, the money was a means to an end. He'd always wanted to help people; it was one of the reasons he'd joined the SEALs. It gave him focus, a purpose. And even a lack of memory about who he was hadn't changed those character traits.

Amy's stomach growled, and she decided she'd had enough of soul-searching. Slipping into the dining hall, she easily spotted Micah, Lucas and the chief of police sharing a small round table. Intensity radiated from them, so she decided to forgo a greeting and just get her food. Fresh fruit, cereal and homemade biscuits beckoned. While fixing her plate, she cast glances their way. The chief finally stood, dwarfing everyone in the room, and walked toward the door, his posture stiff, anger written in his crisp movements.

Hmm. Wonder what Micah said to get that reaction? Probably refused to stay out of the investigation and let the man do his job.

Amy felt a tug on the hem of her shirt, pulling her attention down to the little girl standing next to her. "Hello, little one. How are you this morning?"

Carlita flashed her shy grin, and Amy's heart melted all over again. What a sweet child. Salvador walked over and picked up his sister. She lay her head on his bony shoulder, content to hug her rabbit and watch the world from her perch in Salvador's arms. He kissed the top of her silky dark head, then looked at Amy. "Good morning, *senhorita.* I hope you slept well."

"Sort of." She really didn't want to explain how she tossed and turned for hours after crashing into the bed, only to fall asleep in the wee hours of the morning. "I forgot to set my alarm clock, so I'm running a little late this morning."

Salvador shrugged, sadness flickering through his eyes as he glanced down at the child in his arms. "We are, too. Carlita had another nightmare last night. And the storms always scare her. She hates the thunder."

Amy had noticed the shadows under his eyes. "I'm so sorry." She reached out a finger to trace it down the girl's downy soft cheek. Carlita smiled again and clapped a little hand to cover the spot. Amy laughed. "She's very lucky to have you take care of her."

He turned more solemn. "Yes, I will watch over her the rest of her life. That is a promise I made while standing over my parents' dead bodies."

Amy winced and decided to change the subject. She grabbed a carton of orange juice. "What are your plans for the day?"

"Carlita will go on to school, and I will help on the wing. The frame is finished, the walls are up and the insulation is nearly complete. There is still some wiring to do in the ceiling, but most of that is also finished."

"That sounds like a busy day."

"What will you do today, Miss Amy?"

Amy eyed Micah still seated at the table with Lucas. He was sipping on a cup of coffee, frowning at the doctor across from him.

She drew in a deep breath. "Pray for a miracle."

Micah knew the minute she stepped into the room. His "Amy radar" picked up her signal whenever she came within shouting distance. He had to figure out how to turn that thing off, but it seemed to be a permanent affliction. She'd betrayed him. Well, no, he argued with himself, that had actually been her mother.

It didn't matter. The woman had stolen two and a half years of his life. There was no way he was marrying into that family. Whoa, he pulled his thoughts to a screeching halt. Who said anything about marriage? Where had that come from?

He shook his head, focusing again on Lucas.

The doctor smiled. "You've got it bad, don't you?"

"No. I don't. I can't." Micah speared a wedge of papaya with a fork, then waved it at Lucas. "No way are she and I going to work." He popped the fruit in his mouth and chewed absently.

"I thought your God could do anything."

Micah stared. That was twice Lucas had brought God into a conversation. Narrowing his eyes, he studied the man. "Why is

He 'your' God?" With his two fingers Micah wiggled invisible quotes around the word *your*. "If He's God, He's God, right? Besides you said you believed in Him so that makes Him your God, too."

Lucas blinked. "Whatever. All I'm saying is if you want to have something with the lady, shouldn't you trust in that faith you keep talking about and just go for it?"

"Her mother set me up to die. Falling in love with Amy is out of the question."

That set the good doctor back on his heels a bit. "Oh."

"Yeah. Look, Lucas, I don't want to think about Amy or relationships right now. I just want to know who's out to kill me."

"And I want to help." Amy's soft voice cut in. Micah stiffened, all defenses on high alert. He scanned her face wondering if she'd heard his comment about not falling in love with her, but didn't see any evidence of it.

So much for his "Amy radar" as he hadn't had a blip of a warning that she was right behind him. Instead he saw dark circles that ringed her pretty eyes. She looked worn, tired. His heart wanted to sympathize, but he refused to let it. "What do you think you can do to help, Amy?"

She slid into the empty seat between him

and Lucas. "I just had a thought. Would it be possible that my mother knows you're alive and is somehow orchestrating this from her jail cell?"

Micah gave a start. That was one angle he hadn't thought of. "Jonathas claimed there were posters of me everywhere in town. What if someone recognized me and called her?"

"But who?" Lucas asked.

Amy ran a hand through her dark blond hair, pushing a few stray strands behind her delicate ear. Micah tore his gaze away forcing himself to concentrate on her words. "I don't know. I can't even begin to guess. When I realized it was my mother that was after Cassidy, having her kidnapped from here . . ."

"Whoa, wait, hold on," Micah burst in. "Cassidy? My sister, Cassidy?"

Amy frowned at him. "Yes. I thought you knew all that."

"All what?" Frustration nearly had him climbing the walls.

"Oh, dear," Amy brought a hand to her mouth and whispered behind her fingers. "You mean, you haven't heard that story? I guess I just assumed when you got your memory back, you'd put it all together."

Micah paused, thinking for a moment.

The only story he'd heard about was the one where a few months ago there had been a lady who'd arrived to pick up a child she'd been adopting and had been snatched from the orphanage. Later, she'd escaped her captors with the help of a friend and had shown up back at the orphanage, refusing to leave the country without the child. She'd been so grateful for the help of the relief workers that she'd promised to help rebuild what her captors had damaged. Monthly checks arrived right on schedule.

His eyes went wide. It just hit him. "You mean, my sister, *Cassidy,* is the woman that was kidnapped, and it's because of her the orphanage suffered all this damage? She's the wealthy benefactor? And your mother was involved in that, too?" Shaking his head, he lowered it into his palms and clutched his hair. "Unbelievable."

"Oh, Micah, I'm so sorry."

He shot her an accusing look.

She flinched and held out a beseeching hand. "I wasn't holding out on you, I promise. I never thought I had to tell you that part. I just thought you'd . . . know."

"No," he mumbled without looking up, "no, I didn't know."

Micah gathered his thoughts, looked up and stared at the ceiling. He asked, "Does your mother have the power to have me killed from a jail cell in the U.S.?"

"Probably," she whispered.

A sigh escaped him. "Can you call her and confront her with this?"

"No, no way." Amy jumped up. "I haven't talked to that woman since she's been in jail. I'm not about to start now."

Narrowing his eyes at the distraught Amy, he said, "Actually, I'm not asking. I'm saying you owe me and I want you to call her. Ask her what's going on, and see if you can tell if she's lying or not when she swears she doesn't know what you're talking about."

Lucas stood up next to Amy before she had a chance to argue. "And I'm going to see if the chief can do a little investigating into the family of the man that you shot. Manuel Cruz may be dead, but his legacy, unfortunately, lives on. Then I have to be at the hospital. Keep me updated." He narrowed his eyes at Micah, gathered up his coffee cup and said, "I've got too much invested in you to let someone kill you. I want to help, so let me know what I can do. On that note, I'm going to leave the two of you to work out whatever it is you two need to work out."

The man left, leaving Micah to look at Amy and wonder what he was going to do with her. His heart wanted to love her and push her away at the same time. The inner battle was taking a toll on his emotions.

"So, shall we go find a phone?" He quirked an eyebrow in her direction.

She flinched again. Her sad eyes caught his as she beseeched him, "Don't ask me to do this, please."

Steeling himself, he pointed toward Anna's office. "Ladies first."

ELEVEN

Amy prayed as she led the way down the hall. *Lord, I can't do this. I haven't spoken to her since she went to jail. I avoided her during the trial, refusing to meet her eyes, to acknowledge her presence. How am I supposed to pick up the phone and call her?*

Cassidy's words returned to haunt her. "You'll have to forgive her one day."

God, how do I forgive her? I can't do it. Tears clogged her throat. She swallowed hard. She would have to lean on God.

Amy jerked to a stop. Anna's office door was shut, but a simple knock would bring the woman to open it. Her racing heart slowed; she took a deep breath. A calm settled over her. No, she didn't want to phone her mother. Not yet. She needed to prepare herself, her heart. She looked into Micah's eyes, her breath catching at the look of desolation there. And she was going to add to it. "Micah, I can't do it right now. I need time."

Placing a hand on her arm, he urged, "Time is one thing I may not have, Amy. I need to find out who's after me and why. Calling your mother is a step in the right direction."

Amy backed away from the office, licking her lips and shaking her head. Fear overtook her as she stepped aside. "No, I can't do it. I haven't talked to her since her arrest. She may refuse to talk to me anyway."

The hand gripping her arm squeezed tighter. "Amy . . ."

She jerked from his grip. She wanted to help him, but this was asking too much.

"I thought you wanted to help."

She closed her eyes against the pain in his voice. "I do, Micah, I truly do, but this is . . . it's simply beyond me and . . . I can't."

His eyes went cold. "Fine. I'll call her myself. But a word of advice. If you don't want to help, don't make the offer."

He left without another word. Amy wanted to chase him down and make him understand. *God, I just can't. I know you're my strength, and I truly believe that, given time, I'll be able to make the effort, but right now it's just too soon, too much.* She leaned against the wall, praying, debating. While she was still thinking, Anna popped her head out.

"Oh, Amy. I was just coming to find you. You have a phone call."

Forcing her turbulent emotions under control, she asked, "Who is it?"

Shrugging, Anna waved her into the office. "I don't know. The person just asked to speak to you. Make yourself at home while I run down to the kitchen real quick. I'll be back soon."

Puzzled, Amy stepped into the office and picked up the phone. "Hello?"

"Meet me in three nights." No mistaking that voice. Maria.

Amy sucked in a deep breath, her heart suddenly pounding against her ribs. "Where?"

"At the clearing past Lake Tomalis. I have arranged to get away from the camp once more."

"I don't know where that is."

"The quickest way is to hike through the jungle to the market area. Then you must take the canoe up the river. When you see the red pole with the green flag, get out of the canoe and walk the path. You will find it. It will take you about an hour to get there from the orphanage."

"But how do I contact you if I need to?"

"You won't need to. Lucia is ready. She has agreed to go with you, but there are many in this camp that would kill us both if they find out. Three days."

"Three days. What time?"

"Right before the sun goes down."

"All right. I'll do my best to be there."

"We will only get one chance. If you fail, we all fail."

The phone clicked in her ear. Dizziness assailed her, and for a moment she thought she might pass out. Then common sense knocked her on the head. She was in way too deep. Going alone into the jungle to meet with Maria wasn't an option. She had to have help.

Micah.

God, he's not going to help me. I just refused to help him. *He's really mad at me right now, remember? If I ask him, I'm only setting myself up for rejection, right? Seriously, You think I should ask him? Will he do it?*

Most likely, he'll shake his head in disbelief that I actually had the nerve to ask him.

Setting the phone into the cradle, she decided there was only one way to find out. Determination lifted her chin. Energy quickened her steps as she headed down the hall to the wing under renovation. Jonathas and Salvador painted the new walls a pretty shade of blue. She waved to them, but stayed focused on her objective. She found Micah working on the wires in the ceiling. For a moment she simply stared. He was a beautiful man, scars and all. His movements flowed as he connected wires, clipped the excess and rechecked his work. Amy swallowed hard. She could love him. Easily. If he could only return the sentiment.

"I didn't know you were an electrician, too."

He barely glanced her way, but at least he spoke. "They teach you all kinds of handy things in the Navy."

Amy cleared her throat. "I, uh, wanted to ask you something."

"Ask."

"Could we talk? In private?"

His hands stilled. Shifting on the ladder, he finally looked her in the eye. "What's left to talk about?"

"I need your help."

"My help? You've got nerve, don't you?" Well, she'd called that one, hadn't she? At least he hadn't shaken his head. "Will you please just come down and listen to me? It's not about me and I wouldn't ask if there were any other way."

"Give me five minutes. I'm almost done with this wiring."

A relieved breath escaped her. "Thank you. I'll be waiting in Anna's office."

True to his word, five minutes later, he entered the office through the door she'd left open. Shutting it behind him, he leaned against it, crossing his arms across his chest. "What is it you need?"

What's he thinking? she wondered. *How do I ask him to do this?* Pulling in a fortifying breath, she said, "I have one last thing to tell you." She paced behind Anna's desk and stayed there to keep from throwing herself into his strong arms and begging him to help her. "When I decided to make the trip to Brazil, I had two goals. To find out what God had in mind for my life, what my purpose was, and to find out if I had any family left here. The night you saw me meeting with Maria Morales, I was . . . meeting her for the first time . . . and she told me something about a young girl."

His eyebrow quirked. "Who was this girl?"

She had his attention. That was good. He wasn't snarling at her. Even better. "My cousin, Lucia Morales."

Shock registered for a brief moment, then eyes trained on hers, he asked, "Why are you telling me this now?"

"Because I need your help getting her out of the rebel camp. I had no intention of leaving Brazil this fast, but three days from now, my grandmother Maria has arranged for us to meet and Lucia is going to come with me. She's an American citizen by birth, with a passport and everything. I'll fly home with her to South Carolina where she'll learn what it's like to grow up respected and loved instead of being treated like dirt and possibly sold into prostitution. She's twelve years old. Older than some of the children already . . ." Amy shuddered, unable to finish the sentence. She couldn't imagine that kind of life and had no intention of letting her young cousin — or the other children there — grow up in it. As soon as she and Micah had Lucia and Maria, she'd somehow find a way to convince Maria to reveal the location of the camp. The police would raid it and that would be that. If Maria refused to tell them where it was . . . Amy sighed. She didn't know what she'd do. "I need you to go with me. Help me get her out of there, Micah."

He ran a weary hand over his face, absently tracing the scar. Finally, he shook his head. "No. You need to stay out of the jungle. You're not trained for that kind of thing."

"But you are. You could help me."

"Amy, I understand you want to rescue

her, but face it. How likely is it that Maria is really going to make it happen? It's probably some kind of setup. You've gotten too close to them. You need to let it go. Or —" he waved a hand as though searching for the words "— you've got money. Hire someone, a trained soldier to help you out. I've got contacts. I can call in someone for you, but that's it. I'm done. I refuse to help you put your life in danger."

Stunned at his refusal, she stared at him. His next words threw the rest of her world off its axis.

"I've been thinking about it for a while, but this latest incident with the snakes pretty much cinched the decision. The sooner I'm out of here, the safer everyone will be. For some reason, I've been targeted. Unfortunately, that puts the entire orphanage in danger because, while most of the attempts on my life have been isolated, there's still a chance that staff or, God forbid, a child could wind up in the wrong place. I can't have the death of another . . ."

He broke off and reached a hand behind him. Opening the door, he dropped his bombshell.

"In three days, I'm catching a flight home. I've already booked the ticket."

■ ■ ■ ■

Micah stood at one end of the dock and watched Amy. She sat on the other end, her normal spot, reading her Bible, a new one she'd gotten after her other one had landed in the water with him during the jeep incident. Emotions had him wrung out as he continued to monitor the hurricane that had his family trapped in the Bahamas. The storm had passed, but left devastation in its wake. Cell towers were down, ships were docked, planes grounded. Traveling was virtually impossible in that area.

The chief had called and said that the Cruz family was lying low after the killing of its leader, Manuel. A rogue family member might have gone out on his own to get revenge, but it didn't look as if the Cruzes were the ones responsible for the attempts on his life.

Micah had called Amy's mother and the stunned silence on the other end of the phone told him what he needed to know. She'd had no idea he was alive. Her scream of outrage made him smile out of sheer spite. *Thank You, God, for letting me live, especially if it makes her that mad. Sorry, I know that shouldn't bring me that much satisfaction. Help me work on forgiving her, because, I'll be honest, God, I'm not there yet.*

Deciding to leave the orphanage was one of the toughest decisions he'd ever made. Not only was the mystery of who wanted him dead still there, but he didn't really want to leave Amy. Yes, he was still angry with her, yet in some strange way, he understood. However, convincing himself he had no choice about leaving, the decision was made. Everyone should be safe with him out of the way.

His flight left in the morning, yet he couldn't leave without making sure she wasn't going to do something stupid such as go into the jungle on her own.

And he had to make peace with her. For two days he'd wrestled with God. Pleaded with him to show him what to do. Against his wishes, Amy had ensnared him, caused him to care about her, possibly even love her. She'd looked past not only his physical scars but his emotional ones, as well. She had come to see the real Micah McKnight — saw him with the eyes of Christ. Could he do any less for her?

Could he blame her for her mother's sins? Of course not. But he didn't have to help her put her life in danger, either. When he'd asked God what he should do, he hadn't gotten an answer.

So, as of right now, he was going to straighten things out with her as best he could, then catch a plane in the morning to the U.S. He'd be waiting for his family when they walked in the door from their cruise. And hopefully, with him gone from the orphanage, things would settle down with no more dangerous incidents. It galled him to leave a would-be murderer still out there, but there had been no attempts on anyone else's life, so Micah felt quite sure he was the only target. And if he removed the target, maybe this person would go away.

Turning his attention back to Amy, he was struck by her vulnerability. Her shoulders shook with the effort to hold back her sobs, and his heart shuddered in sympathy. All that she'd been through played through his mind and he just couldn't hold on to his anger anymore. Forgiving Juanita Morales, aka Cecelia Graham, would take a little longer, but mentally, Micah was willing to admit that Amy was innocent of any wrongdoing. He just had to convince his heart.

He walked the length of the dock, stopping behind her. Sure that she'd felt the vibration of his approach, heard his footfalls on the wood, he didn't bother to announce himself. She knew it was him. He knelt beside her.

Without looking at him she asked, "What do you want, Micah? My heart's already full of all the holes you can shoot in it. Any more and it'll be beyond repair. Do you think you could have a little mercy?"

He blew out a breath. "Okay, I deserved that."

"Yes, you did. But I'll heal — again. God will get me through all this and I'll be fine — again."

"I'm sorry, Amy."

That brought her up short. She stilled, her gaze fixed on the water. "Excuse me?"

"I'm sorry. I shouldn't have blamed you for your mother's actions. You're completely innocent in all this and I . . ."

"No, I'm not innocent. I should have told you right away your identity."

"What's the real reason you didn't? Somehow, I think there's more to it than what you've told me so far."

"Well, I guess because by the time I realized who you were, we were already growing close."

At this statement, Micah felt as if someone had reached into his chest to twist his heart. He tried to cover it by asking, "And?"

"And," she drew the word out, "I knew

that if you remembered who you were, you'd remember me, thus remembering how I was before I became a Christian. I suppose, subconsciously, I was trying to buy time."

"Time for what?"

She finally peeked at him through red-rimmed eyes. At least the tears had stopped. He reached up and trailed his thumb down a damp cheek, wincing when she turned her head away. He let his hand drop.

"Time for you to get to know me as I am now. I'm a different woman than the one you grew up with all those years ago. I know you secretly thought I was a brat." She gave a hiccupping chuckle. "And you were right. I was." She bit her lip, looked across the water, then back up at him. "But I wanted you to see the different me. I didn't want you to remember the bratty me. Very selfish of me, I admit. For that, I owe you an apology. I truly am so very sorry. And, of course, it's very hard to admit your mother is a murderer . . . especially to the person she set up to die. The pain . . ."

Micah closed his eyes, then risked settling his arm across her shoulder. When she didn't push him away, he pulled her closer and tucked her into his side. "You know, you're the one that made me realize I have

219

a relationship with Christ. Even before I got my memory back, I was searching for Him, wanting to know Him the way you do. I realize now He was always there. And while I couldn't remember Him, He remembered me. I think God used your arrival here to let me know that." Then he said abruptly, "Come home with me."

She pulled away. "What?"

Grabbing her hand, excitement started to flow through him. "Come home with me. Let's start over. We'll get to know each other just as we are now. No looking back. No remembering the past. Just now. You and me."

Before the last word left his mouth, he wondered where his filters were. What had he just done? Could he marry the daughter of the woman who betrayed him? What kind of legacy would that be for their children? After all his agonizing, he had blurted that out. What an idiot.

A bittersweet smile crossed her face. "That would be wonderful, wouldn't it?"

"So, you'll do it?"

Shaking her head, she said, "No, right now your hurt is too fresh. You need time to heal. But it's a nice dream."

Deflated, yet relieved, he muttered, "Yeah."

They sat in silence for about five minutes with Micah still holding her hand. Finally, she asked, "So what now?"

"Are you still intent on meeting your grandmother and cousin?"

"I have to, Micah."

"I was afraid of that. I'll find you a guide."

"I'd appreciate it."

He gestured to her Bible. "What does God have to say this morning?"

She shrugged. "I don't know. I hadn't gotten around to the listening part yet. I was too busy begging Him to help me convince you I meant you no harm and that I had nothing to do with my mother's schemes."

"Well, it worked. I believe you."

"Thanks." A fresh tear slid down her cheek, and his heart nearly snapped in two.

He pulled her against him. "Amy, I can't stand it. I want to be with you, I just don't know how to get past . . ."

Soft fingers covered his lips. Her mouth trembled as she said, "Go home, Micah. It hurts too much. Maybe one day, God will work it out, but until then . . ."

He leaned his forehead against her, then shifted to kiss her. A lingering kiss that spoke of unfulfilled longing, the desire to forgive, yet included a painful goodbye. Finally, she pushed him away. "Go."

He went.

Amy crammed another water bottle into her bulging pack. Zipping it shut, she thought about Micah and his promise to find her a guide. She thought he might tell her at the last minute he'd take her, but he hadn't. Disappointment sat heavy on her heart.

Instead, he'd left her a message that Romero, the relief worker who'd originally met her at the airport upon her arrival to Brazil, had agreed to lead her into the jungle. Unfortunately, Romero had come down with some kind of stomach virus and wasn't going anywhere except to bed. And Micah, unaware of Romero's plight, had said his goodbyes to the children and staff, climbed into a taxi and disappeared down the rutted road. Amy had watched silently from afar, pleading with the Lord to change Micah's mind.

But it wasn't to be and now she was stuck with a decision to make. She could either go on her own, try to find someone else to go with her or she could not go at all. But that last one really wasn't an option. No, somehow, someway, she had to be there to get Lucia and get out. Anna was reluctantly in on the plan, but promised to do what she could to back Amy up. Anna had even made a few calls trying to find a replacement guide, but with no luck.

Amy prayed, paced, prayed some more. What should she do? A glance at her watch told her she needed to get moving soon. There was no way she wanted to be stuck on the river in the middle of the night. Although if they were supposed to meet at dusk, the sun would be sinking fast. She packed a heavy-duty flashlight just in case. If only there was some way to contact Maria to change the meeting. What would happen if Maria and Lucia showed up and Amy didn't? They'd have to go back to the camp to face possible death.

Unable to allow that, Amy resolved to do what she could and if she died trying, well, at least she was ready to meet God. Not that she was in any hurry, but if it happened . . .

Oh, Micah, why couldn't you help me? She actually couldn't believe he'd been so selfish as to just dump her like this. His hurt had obviously clouded his thinking. This was so unlike him. And the fact that he could leave with his attempted murders still unsolved . . . She shook her head. Micah had apparently reached his breaking point.

Checking the side pocket for the gun she'd managed to convince Anna she needed, she gave it a comforting pat, then closed the pocket. She slung the heavy pack over her shoulder, opened the door to her room and stepped out into the hall.

"Where are you going, Miss Amy?"

Amy jumped at the quiet question.

"Hey there, Salvador. I'm . . . taking a little trip into the jungle."

"Why?"

She didn't really want to get into it with him. "I just have some thinking to do and need to get away for a while."

"That is not safe, Miss."

"I know, but it's something I have to do." Amy flashed him a distracted smile. She needed to get going. She only had a few hours of sunlight left. Plenty of time, as Maria had said the trip should only take about an hour, but Amy wanted to make sure she gave herself extra time in case she got lost. "I'll see you when I get back, okay?"

"No, I will go with you."

"Salvador, I can't ask you to do that."

"You are going into the jungle. You need someone to be there to help you."

She really did, but Salvador? Could she ask him to do something that might be really dangerous? The jungle itself held its own dangers, of course, but her situation held threats of another kind. The human kind.

"That's not a good idea. I can't ask you to do that."

"I will just follow you to make sure, then. That way you are not asking."

Amy gave a mental groan. She really had to get going. "But you don't have any supplies or anything, and I don't know that I have enough for the both of us."

"Please do not worry about me. Give me five minutes to get some things from my room."

Giving in, Amy decided it was better to be able to have him in plain sight rather than have him follow her and then to be constantly looking over her shoulder worrying about him. Another door down the hall snapped shut and Amy looked up to see Jonathas staring at her, she gave a little wave. Then Salvador stepped out of the room with a pack similar to hers slung over his shoulder.

On their way out the door, anticipation, fear and worry tumbled around inside her. Could she do this? She hated to admit it, but Salvador's presence brought comfort. A false sense of security? Maybe. *Please God, go before us, lead the way. Keep us safe. And be with Micah. He's hurting. Show him Your love and let him feel Your presence.*

He couldn't do it. Micah had changed his flight twice already, delaying the inevitable, and security was beginning to give him some funny looks. He couldn't just leave her like that. Micah groaned at the battle going on inside his soul. The desire to get away from everything and everyone, go home, crawl into bed and sleep for a month overwhelmed him. But he couldn't. And yet, if he stayed at the orphanage, would he be putting people he cared about in danger? Right now, no one had been hurt in all of the mishaps aimed at him.

Deep down he wanted — no, needed — to stay.

A chill shook him. Micah hadn't made a big deal about his departure because he had been afraid if the would-be killer found out he was leaving, the assassin would be pushed into making a last-ditch effort to get rid of him. Before he'd left, he'd pressed a note into Amy's hand with instructions to give it to Salvador and Carlita. His apology for not saying goodbye in person. Then he'd said goodbye to Amy and Anna, climbed into the taxi and sped away. He'd call Lucas from the airport.

The look on Amy's face when he'd left

still haunted him. While her lips remained silent, her eyes had begged him to stay, yet flashed their understanding of why he had to leave. The cabbie had noticed the silent exchange and had shaken his head until Micah wanted to throttle the man. And each time the man had said, "I turn around now, *sim?* You go kiss woman and make up, yes?" Micah responded with a short, "No."

And so the cabbie left him standing on the sidewalk in front of the entrance to the airport, where he finally made it all the way down the ramp to the airplane. And here he sat, trying to figure out where his anxiety was coming from. The Cruz family wasn't after him, as everyone still thought he was dead; no one had recognized him from the posters around town. Micah was ninety-nine percent sure it wasn't Amy's mother. Romero would escort Amy to meet her grandmother, offering excellent protection should anything go wrong. Everything should be fine. Right?

Wrong. Why was he so antsy about leaving?

Awareness slowly crept up, working its way into his brain until it was crystal clear.

There was no way he could entrust Amy's safety to someone else. Romero was a good guy, but Micah wasn't willing to bet the guy would give his life to keep Amy safe. Micah swallowed hard, realizing he would. *Okay, God, I got it. I'm supposed to be there for her.*

That realization propelled him from the airplane seat. The door was closing. "Wait!" Hurtling himself down the aisle, he stopped to briefly explain to the stewardess, "I'm an idiot. I need off this plane."

She eyed him suspiciously. He blurted, "I left something here."

"What?"

"The woman I love."

She opened the door.

TWELVE

Even in the middle of October, the temperatures stayed in the mid to high eighties. Sweat poured from both Amy and Salvador as they trudged through the overgrown jungle. Amy swiped a mosquito away from her face, and asked, "Where's the canoe, Salvador?"

"Only a little farther." Fortunately, Salvador had thought to bring a machete. He used it with skill, slicing his way through the thick vines. Amy's legs shuddered at the demands she was making on them.

A vine snarled her ankle, tripping her. She landed with a thud, scraping her left elbow. Salvador stopped and looked back. "Are you all right?"

Amy pulled herself up with a grunt. "Fine." She waved him on. "Don't worry about me, I'm coming." Disregarding her assurances, he reached down to pull her up. She stumbled against him and he steadied her. Salvador looked behind. "Do you think *senhor* Micah will come looking for us? He would not like that you are in the jungle."

"No," Amy said, grief ripping at her insides, "no, I don't think we'll have to worry about Micah. He's flown home to the United States."

"What?" exclaimed Salvador. "Why?"

"Because he was worried the person trying to kill him would miss and accidentally hurt someone else."

Anger contorted Salvador's features. "He didn't tell me."

"Oh," Amy patted her right front pocket, pulled out Micah's note and handed it to Salvador. "Here. He asked me to give you this. Don't be upset with him, Salvador. I didn't want him to leave, either, but I know why he did it."

Without another word, Salvador read the letter, crumpled it up and slid it into his pocket. The anger remained etched on his face. Amy's heart hurt for him. One more slap, one more person he felt had let him down in his life. It wasn't fair, but Micah had only done it to protect him, as well as every other person at the orphanage. One day Salvador would realize that.

They continued on for another fifteen minutes, although to Amy it seemed to be hours. Panting, she leaned over to grip her knees. "Hey, Salvador, there's some canoes." Four little wooden boats sat on the edge of the water, pulled up far enough to keep from being swept away. They crept closer keeping a watchful eye on the surrounding bushes.

Okay, God, now what? Do I continue with this? I don't want Salvador in danger. He's gotten me this far. Can I go the rest of the way by myself? I mean, of course You'll be with me, but . . .

"You are ready, Ms. Amy? We go on the river now, yes?"

Caution.

Amy sat on an exposed root. "Not yet, Salvador. I want to be really careful. I also want you to return to the orphanage." She patted her satellite phone in her hip pocket for reassurance.

"No. I am not leaving yet. We need to get into the canoe and go up the river."

"How far is Lake Tomalis from here?"

Salvador hesitated, glanced around. "About four miles. Should take about an hour to get there."

"I want to watch for a while. Let's just sit here a bit and be careful." Make sure she wasn't being played the fool. Maria might be her grandmother, but Amy wasn't dumb enough to trust the woman any further than she could throw her.

Blowing out a huge sigh, Salvador sat down, obviously disgruntled. He fingered the machete, as though he itched to get moving. Amy passed him a bottle of water.

It seemed to take double the time, but Micah finally arrived back at the orphanage. Too late to stop Amy or go with her. He'd have to find a way to follow her trail — or find someone who knew where Lake Tomalis was located. Micah had a general idea, but wasn't exactly sure he could find it without getting lost and wasting precious time.

Jonathas.

The boy was familiar with this part of the jungle and beyond. Maybe he could help. Micah headed into the main building, striding quickly down the hallway that led to Jonathas's room.

"Micah!"

Anna's startled call stopped him in his tracks. He spun and sprinted back to her. Before she could ask, he said, "I couldn't leave her, Anna. How long ago did she leave?"

"About thirty minutes ago. I begged her not to go, especially after Romero got sick and couldn't go with her."

Terror sucked the air from his lungs. "She went alone?"

Ignoring his bellow, she waved her satellite phone at him. "I tried to stop her, but you know Amy. The minute she calls me, I'm to report to the chief where to raid the camp. She's so concerned about the children being raised there, but she wanted the chance to get her cousin and grandmother out first."

His jaw clenched. "So she thinks her grandmother should get off without facing charges like every one of those murdering rebels."

"No, but Amy wants a chance to talk her grandmother into turning herself in. She's hoping for leniency if Maria's willing to give the authorities information leading to the arrest of some of the most wanted rebels. I'm not holding out much hope, though. Amy doesn't realize . . ." Anna bit her lip and Micah glanced at the time.

"We can worry about this later. I need to find Amy before she meets up with Maria. There's no way Amy can be sure the woman would keep her word. If Romero were with her, I wouldn't be so worried." He punched in her satellite phone number. It never rang, just went straight to voice mail. She had either turned her phone off, or the battery was dead. He snapped his phone shut, barely leashing his anger and fear.

Anna said, "I think Salvador went with her. I never would have let him go if I'd known, but Carlita started wandering the orphanage and appeared to be looking for her brother without any success. Normally, he's right there when she goes looking for him. This time, though . . ."

He groaned. "All right, I'm going after her. I've got my satellite phone. I'll keep trying her and will call you when I know something. If Amy calls you, you call me and vice versa. Deal?"

"Deal. Be careful, Micah. I don't want to lose another person I care about. You, or Amy."

"Where's Jonathas? I'm going to need his help."

"Check his room. I saw him go in a little while ago. He seemed kind of agitated, and he ignored me when I asked him if something was wrong." She shrugged. "I gave him his space. He knows he can come to me if he needs to."

Micah spun on his heel and headed for the boy's room. A quick, hard rap brought no response, but the door swung slowly inward. Micah flipped on the light switch.

"Jonathas?"

Nothing.

Stepping into the room, Micah took in the almost compulsive cleanliness. Wow, his mom would've loved it if he'd kept his room like this as a teenager. The door must not have latched well when Jonathas exited the last time. Anna said he'd been agitated; maybe he'd left in a hurry.

About to turn and leave, the overhead fan Micah had turned on when he entered caused a paper to flutter to the floor. Muttering about wasting time, he bent over to pick it up and stopped. It was a picture of Manuel Cruz. What was Jonathas doing with a picture of the man Micah had killed?

Unease crept over him. He looked at the stack of papers on top of the dresser, reached up and pulled them down to look at them. The second picture was of him and Amy at the picnic. The look in her eye as she gazed up at him said a lot. He'd investigate that later.

What concerned him right now was Amy's face had been X'd out with a red marker. He flipped through them, each one making his heart beat faster. The pictures consisted of almost all of the staff, a lot of whom had red X's on their faces. The one of Salvador and Carlita stumped him. No X, just a big circle around Salvador. Another picture showed Romero working on the wing. His face, too, had been X'd out. Then Anna.

What was going on?

And then he came across one with Manuel Cruz and Jonathas, sitting together in front of a pool. Manuel had his arm around Jonathas with a big grin on his face. Jonathas had a rather stony expression, as though he hadn't wished to have his picture taken. A young boy sat in front of them playing with some pool toys. Micah gasped. Jonathas was Manuel's son! Had Jonathas been trying to kill Micah all this time? Of course! He'd been the one to recognize Micah from the pictures posted in town — and come to the orphanage to find him.

And when Micah left, out of his reach, Jonathas had gone for the next best thing, the woman Micah loved — Amy.

Prayers whispered on his lips as he flipped to the next item. His breath whooshed out in shock; the last picture nearly singed his fingers. He was staring at his own face from over two years ago, a fax sent from a number in South Carolina to a number Micah would go to his grave with, the number for the man Micah had been undercover to expose. The date at the top was two days before the mission and had been sent to

Manuel Cruz. How had Jonathas come to have this in his possession?

As Micah tumbled the information around in his mind, he realized one thing. Amy was trapped. In front of her was a woman that might very well kill her as look at her and behind her, closing in fast, was a teen who probably wanted to see her dead.

Micah bolted to Anna's office, offered a quick, garbled explanation, grabbed a gun and headed for the jungle.

Amy could sense Salvador's restlessness beside her. The boy was ready to move and so was she, but she hadn't hurried up to this moment and didn't want to start now. Taking things slowly might just be the thing to keep them alive. "Just a few more minutes, okay? I just think we're supposed to sit."

"I am tired of sitting. Let's go."

"It seems kind of silly, doesn't it? I just have a feeling . . ."

"No one has come around the canoes. They are for public use, anyway."

She chewed her lip for a moment. "Just a few more moments, then we'll go. All right?"

Salvador gave a grunt and fell silent, his eyes darting around the jungle, keeping watch.

Ten minutes later, with no activity happening, Amy said, "Well, I don't see any reason to keep waiting. Let's go."

The two headed down to the edge of the river where Salvador's head swiveled, taking in everything around him. Amy was touched by his obvious concern for her safety. She had left the orphanage in plenty of time, so right now she was in no danger of being late to the meeting.

She just wanted to be careful, take her time. She hoped Salvador would be willing to go along with that. He seemed extra nervous, but she attributed that to the situation. Not exactly relaxed herself, she took a deep breath, said another prayer and told herself it would be all right. Wouldn't it?

Even if Micah would croak if he were aware of what she was doing. The pain of thinking about him zinged through her; she wondered if it would ever fade. With her right hand, she reached for the satellite phone in her front pocket. She could call him. Just one last time. By now he had probably landed somewhere in Mexico on his way to the U.S.

She patted her flat pocket, horror pulling her to a stop. It was gone!

"What is it?" Salvador frowned as he stepped up beside her. "My phone is gone.

It must have slipped out of my pocket!"
Frantic, she searched the area around her.
Unfortunately, there was no time to go back
to the place where she'd fallen and search.
She'd just have to rely on Salvador and God
to keep her alive.

Salvador maneuvered the larger canoe to
the water. Now, he stood holding it, the
machete strapped across his back. Amy
forged ahead. No turning back now. She
headed for the canoe offering a few more
prayers as she slung a leg over the side.

Please, Jesus, keep us safe.

Micah knew he sounded like an elephant as
he crashed through the jungle. The gun sat
snug against the middle of his back, the
machete he'd grabbed as an afterthought
hung across his shoulder. He hadn't had
time to grab the rest of the supplies he
normally would have taken on a jaunt into
the trees, but all he could picture was Amy
in trouble. The image kept his adrenaline
pumping in time with his footsteps. His
SEAL training returned full force. His
favorite mode of travel was water, however,
he felt right at home in this situation, too.
SEALs trained for everything, were taught
to expect the unexpected and to be ready
for anything.

Even land combat.

And if, when, he caught up with Jonathas, he'd make the boy share supplies with him — at least until he had him back in Tefe locked up in a cell. Fury aided his tromp. Adrenaline surged. Thoughts of Amy swirled even while he kept a vigilant eye on the jungle around him. Getting careless now wouldn't help anyone.

She'd been an unusually beautiful child. At first a little shy, but once she got to know you, a chatterbox without an off switch. Then a wild party girl, a teenager with an attitude, who refused to let the hurting, neglected child she'd been show through.

Never a dull moment with her. Micah had agonized every time she and Cassidy had disappeared for a night of partying. He'd followed them a couple of times and confronted them. They'd both blasted him, incensed that he'd butted in on their fun. He told them he didn't care; he was going to look after Cassidy even if that meant she hated him for the rest of her life. Of course, looking after Cassidy also meant looking after Amy. Later, Amy's wild side calmed down and she soon followed Cassidy's decision to accept Christ, turning her life around.

Micah shook his head and followed the

path recently cut by a machete. Salvador had done the hard part of clearing the path, which allowed Jonathas to easily follow in his footsteps. Fortunately, that also made it easy for Micah to do the same.

And Jonathas wouldn't be expecting him.

He could follow the path almost absently, focusing his senses on the jungle around him. He traveled swiftly yet more carefully, to the point of being silent, and almost fell over Jonathas. Fortunately, the boy was facing in the other direction, crouched down and peering through the leaves in front of him. Micah stopped, backing up until he felt well hidden.

For a few moments, he simply watched Jonathas. What was he doing? Biding his time? Did he see Amy and Salvador ahead? Stealthily, Micah pulled the pistol from his waistband, hefting it in his right hand, comforted by the feel of the cold steel. Did Jonathas have a weapon? It was highly likely. Assessing the situation, Micah decided it was now or never. "Psst."

Jonathas whirled at the sound, eyes probing the jungle growth. Micah stepped into the boy's line of vision. "Hello, Jonathas. Or should I say, Cruz Junior?"

Fear flared in the teen's eyes before it dimmed to dull acceptance. "How did you figure it out?"

"I went looking for you. I found a bunch of pictures instead."

His Adam's apple bobbed twice. "Oh. I left those on my dresser, didn't I?"

Micah stepped closer. "Yeah, you did."

Solemn black eyes squinted at him. Jonathas said, "I wanted to tell you."

"Really? Well, I kind of understand why you didn't. That would have messed up the plan to get rid of me, wouldn't it?"

Confusion drew Jonathas's eyebrows together. "Get rid of you? No, *senhor,* I had no desire to get rid of you. I was protecting you."

Micah gave a short laugh. "I don't think our definitions of *protection* would match up."

"Seriously, when I saw your picture posted all over town, I finally recognized you in spite of the scars. I remembered you from my father's house. I thought you were one of *them.*" He spat the word.

"How come I don't remember seeing you? Not ever?" Micah lowered the gun, still wary, but willing to listen. The truth shining in Jonathas's eyes was hard to discount.

"I did not live with my father. I only visited when he demanded it. And even then, I did my best to stay out of sight. My mother died five years ago and I've lived with her mother, my grandmother, since then. My mother's family did not approve of my father — or his line of work."

"So how did you recognize me — and what made you realize that I wasn't one of the bad guys?"

"Often when visiting my father, I would steal into his office looking for evidence to give to the authorities. I hated the man and wanted him out of my life forever. I figured the only way that was going to happen was if I had something even the police could not deny. So, when I knew he was in a meeting or otherwise occupied, I would go looking."

"And?"

"And —" Jonathas sucked in a deep breath "— I was hiding there in the office when you came in one day to give my father the money to put in the safe. His office was very big, with many hiding places. This time, I hid in the bathroom and peeked through the door during your transaction. When you were finished, you turned around and had this look of disgust on your face, like the whole thing was something you wished not to do."

Very perceptive kid. But he needed to get going. Amy still wasn't out of danger. "So why are you following Amy?"

"Because I don't trust Salvador."

That set him back. "Why?"

"Very sneaky, that one. I have been watching him. Not right in the head." Jonathas tapped his forehead to emphasize his point. "He is the one who was mostly involved in setting up for the picnic. He worked with the dunking booth. I also saw him put something into Romero's coffee this morning. At the time, I didn't think anything about it, I thought he was just helping to serve, like he often does. Later, as I was helping clean up, I found the package. It was some kind of powdered laxative. You know, the kind of thing that makes you . . ."

Micah held up a hand. "I get the picture."

"So, when Salvador and Amy left the orphanage, I followed them." He looked back over his shoulder. "We must go. They are getting into the canoe."

Amy looked back over her shoulder as Salvador gave the canoe a shove into the brown water. Uneasiness rippled through her. Out on the open water, she felt exposed — and watched. Shivering in spite of the heat, she scanned the edge of the trees but saw nothing.

Salvador hopped into the little wooden

seat in front of her, grabbing up a paddle and offering the second one to Amy. She glanced at her watch glad to see they still had a good hour before the meeting. Arriving early seemed to be the smart thing to do. If anything about this meeting could be considered smart.

As they drifted with the river, Amy's thoughts turned to Micah. They always seemed to turn to him. Salvador rested the machete across his thighs, yet his eyes never stopped moving. They passed one other canoe heading in the opposite direction. Amy watched the riders paddle against the current. It was possible, just a lot of work. Her arms already ached thinking about the return trip.

The river wasn't usually a busy place this time of evening, but it wasn't unusual to see other canoes or people washing their laundry at the edge of the river.

"How far do you think we've gone?"

Salvador jerked as though he'd been deep in thought. "Oh, about a mile, maybe."

The farther they went, the more nervous she became. Was it too late to turn around? No, but if she did, then Maria and Lucia might die. She'd keep going. If she could put her reason for being on the river out of her mind, she might actually enjoy the trip.

The jungle was gorgeous, teeming with life. Even the mosquitoes didn't bother her terribly, of course, she'd sprayed on bug repellent. She had her stash in her backpack for the return trip.

Two pink dolphins cavorted near the canoe, and Amy gasped. This wasn't the first time she'd seen them, but it was the first time for an up close observation. They were spectacular. She watched them until they disappeared into their dolphin world.

"Okay, Miss Amy. It's your turn to go swimming."

Amy turned her attention to Salvador — and gasped. Only this time not in awe. Disbelief made her blink. The boy held the machete pointed at her chest.

"W-w-what?" she stammered.

"Out," he demanded.

Amy looked into his eyes and shuddered at the coldness there. Stunned, she stared, unable to respond or move as he'd ordered. "Salvador?" she whispered.

"Jump. You will not suffer long."

Thirteen

Micah kept his eyes peeled on the canoe in front of them. Relief at finding Amy in one piece warred with the worry of what he would do if something happened before he caught up with them.

Part of him just wanted to follow and rescue her, should she need it. The other part of him wanted to catch up to let her know he was there. Jonathas rowed with steady even strokes. "Slow down a little. I don't think I want them to know we're here yet. If you're wrong and Salvador is innocent, we've got nothing to worry about."

"I'm not wrong." Jonathas set the paddle across his lap. "*Senhor,* what were you doing that day in my father's office giving him money?"

"I was undercover. That was government money, trying to set your father up. We were hoping the bills would turn up in a human-trafficking sting we were working. We also had guys on a separate, yet connected, undercover mission with well-known traffickers whom your father financed — in return for a huge payoff, of course. With your father's fingerprints on the money and with it in the hands of the human traffickers, we would have had him on that. We wanted him for murder, but he never did that dirty work, so we were willing to take what we could get while searching for more evidence. Of course, we got ratted out before we could pull it all together."

Jonathas ran a hand through hair that could use a cut. He nodded, "Yes, I was there that day."

Shock zipped through Micah. "You were there? How'd you get out alive?"

A small, humorless smile crossed Jonathas's lips. "I told you my father's house had many hiding places. One such place was a bomb shelter built underneath the mansion. I was outside on the far end when the first explosion went off."

"What made you come back into the house?"

"My little brother was there."

Micah went weak in the knees. The boy who'd died. "I'm sorry. I had him, then the bomb went off. I remember his hand slipping out of mine and the bomb going off.

248

After that . . ." Closing his eyes, Micah pictured the moment. *The explosion, his hand gripping air, the blinding pain in his head, then nothing.*

"I know. I found you while I was looking for Mattie. He was hiding in the fireplace. My father's money saved the son he tried to kill. That rock fireplace is still standing and Mattie is living with my grandmother now."

For a moment, it didn't register. Then awareness shook him harder than a volcano in full eruption. "He's alive?"

"Sim."

Swallowing hard, Micah let the answer flow through his entire being. *Oh, thank You, Jesus.* The mission had been a success after all. The child was now living with people who loved him.

"What about Mattie's mother?"

"I don't know who she is or how to contact her. For now, Mattie is fine. Anyway, after the second explosion, I ran upstairs from the underground shelter and found Mattie crying in the fireplace. You were lying there, covered in blood." Jonathas swallowed hard. "I thought you were dead, so I grabbed Mattie and ran for the door, but we couldn't get out. I thought the only way out was back down through the bomb shelter. When we got out, my father and another man were fighting. You were on the ground not too far away. I still don't know how you managed to crawl out of the house, but you did."

Briefly, Micah wondered why the bomb shelter hadn't been on the blueprints they'd had before going in. Someone messed up somewhere.

"That bomb shelter. That's how your father got out, too, isn't it?"

Jonathas nodded. "He never knew I knew about it. But I learned how to play 'spy' at a very young age."

As a matter of survival, no doubt.

Micah had no clue how he'd gotten out of the house. He supposed that was one memory that may stay lost to him forever.

"Why did you X out their faces? In the pictures?"

"I was trying to figure who was making all the attempts on your life. When I decided they were innocent, I X'd them out. It finally came down to Salvador. And after I saw what he did to Romero this morning, that kind of was the final clue." His attention was diverted. "Hey," he said suddenly, "what are they doing?"

Micah squinted against the sun. Amy stood precariously in the canoe, her hands gesturing wildly. Salvador held the machete pointed at her. Micah's blood ran cold. Time to intervene. He grabbed a paddle and ordered, "Row, Jonathas."

"What are you doing?" Amy cried. "Why?" The machete poked her in the stomach but she had nowhere to go except over the side. Her eyes widened as Salvador pulled her satellite phone from his pocket. "One of the many skills I learned living on the streets." He'd picked her pocket! Dread thudded through her as he tossed it over the side into the water.

Gulping, she begged, "Tell me what I've done to make you want to kill me."

"Micah is in love with you. He is responsible for the deaths of my family. Now, I will kill his hope for a family."

Amy felt her jaw drop. "How is Micah responsible for your family's death?"

"After you are gone, eaten by the piranhas, the man will suffer greatly — just as Carlita and I have suffered. I stood by his bedside hoping he would die, even tried to smother him with the pillow, but *you* arrived." He hissed his frustration. "And he recovered. So I shot the darts in the window, but he was lucky." His brow crinkled. "I still cannot believe I missed."

"That was you?" Amy's world spun. "No,

but . . ."

"And then you were talking about it on your walk. I was in the bushes and was going to finish the job, but couldn't get a good shot. I was afraid to try again. If I missed again, he would catch me."

Well, thank God for that. She stalled. "What about the jeep on the dock. How did you arrange that?"

He shrugged. "I know Jonathas's morning routine. I simply went first to the place where he takes care of the cows. When he wasn't looking, I got in the jeep and drove it to the dock where I saw him with you. I waited until he was alone, then wedged the gas pedal down. Very easy."

"And the snakes?" Anger made her shake.

Salvador said, "My pets. I was saving them for something special." His face hardened. "But that failed, too. But now I have you here. I cannot let you take Carlita to the United States. She is my only remaining family. And Micah will suffer when he realizes you have died because of him." He looked up, his eyes going wide. Whatever he saw scared him. Looking back at Amy he said, "Jump. You must jump!" He jabbed the machete even harder, the tip nicking through her shirt and grabbing skin.

She shrieked, stumbled back, her calves

252

catching the edge of the canoe. Then she felt herself hitting the water.

"Amy!" Micah hollered. Salvador looked up at his yell, grabbed a paddle and started rowing. "Jonathas, paddle after Amy, we need to get her into the canoe."

He'd seen the machete being jabbed toward her stomach and her fall into the water. He prayed she wasn't hurt too badly. They were far enough from shore that if she were bleeding, the piranhas would have a field day. He shuddered at the thought.

Amy bobbed to the surface and immediately struck out for shore. Micah prayed like he'd never prayed before as he yanked the paddle through the water. Right now, in October, it was considered late in the dry season. The fish would be hungry.

"Swim, Amy, swim," he whispered.

She jerked, went under, surfaced, then stroked harder. Micah noticed the red tinge in the water around her and felt panic nearly explode his pounding heart. *Please, Jesus.* Salvador was a dot on the river in front of them. Frustration raged. He wanted to find a way to get to the teen, but Amy came first.

She seemed to spasm again. Finally, Micah pulled alongside her. Concentrating so hard on swimming, she didn't realize he was beside her. He reached out and grabbed her arm. She came up fighting.

The canoe rocked, tipped dangerously. "It's me! Let me pull you in."

"Micah! Get me out of here, please," she sobbed as she gripped his hand.

Jonathas kept them balanced while Micah hauled her over the side. She flung her arms around his waist and wept while Jonathas looked on with wide eyes. The boy's glance took in her drenched and bloodied form while Micah silently asked if she was all right. Jonathas pulled his backpack from under him. Grabbing a first-aid kit, he tossed it to Micah.

With his free hand, Micah patted her back, stroked her hair, whatever he could think of to offer silent comfort. She'd been through an ordeal, she deserved a good cry. He was even okay with her bleeding on him as long as she was safe.

Sniffing, she finally pulled away. "I'm okay." She gasped, "Salvador! He'll head for the orphanage to get Carlita. We have to call Anna."

Micah tossed his satellite phone to Jonathas. "Call Anna and fill her in." He pressed a hand on Amy's shoulder. "Sit down on my pack and let me see your legs."

"My legs?"

"Yeah, I think you've got a few bites there."

"I thought something was stinging me."

"Piranhas."

She shuddered. "Probably attracted by the blood from my stomach."

Micah tried to keep the rage from his voice, his tone neutral. "How hard did he jab you?"

With a wince, she pulled the hem of her shirt up to reveal a small but gaping wound right above her belly button. In Micah's opinion, it needed a couple of stitches. He grabbed antibiotic ointment from the kit. She slathered some on her finger from the tube and covered the gash, then placed two butterfly Band-Aids over it to hold the edges of skin together.

"You'll need to take some antibiotics for a couple of weeks. That water is nasty, and you don't want to risk getting an infection." He kept his voice even as he went to work on her bites.

"I know." She hitched her breath and bit her lip as he probed, medicated and bandaged.

Blue jeans had offered her some protection from the three bites on her legs. She had two on her upper right arm. They weren't the worst he'd ever seen, thank

God. Instead, it was almost as if the fish were giving her little test nibbles to see if she were worth attacking. Contrary to what television shows and movies portrayed, piranhas didn't normally attack prey larger than themselves. In fact, most of the time they swam away in fright.

However, the scent of blood would set them off, causing them to devour a larger animal — or human — in a relatively quick period of time. He shuddered at the thought. What if he hadn't gotten off that plane? Would Jonathas have been there to save her? He pushed the thought away, unable to bear pondering it.

Amy trembled, but kept her lips clamped tight. Micah could tell the bites stung, but other than a quick indrawn breath every once in a while, she never voiced a complaint.

Jonathas shut the phone, handing it back to Micah. "Miss Anna said she will contact the chief right away and have him waiting when Salvador shows up. She also will keep Carlita with her."

"All right, let's head back to the orphanage. We'll call Lucas on the way back so he can meet us there to check you over."

"No!" Amy protested. "I still have to meet my grandmother and Lucia."

Micah's jaw dropped. "You're still planning on that?"

"Well, of course. If I don't, I may as well sign their death warrants. Please, Micah, we still have time. Get me to Lake Tomalis."

Amy stared up at Micah desperate to portray the fact that if she had to jump back into the piranha-infested river in order to reach her destination, she'd do it.

Tight-lipped, Micah didn't say another word. Instead, he passed a paddle to Jonathas, grabbing the second one for himself. Relief settled on Amy's tense shoulders. Slowly she let out the breath she'd been holding, shivering in spite of the heat. Hopefully, the sun would dry her out before it went down. If not, it was going to be a chilly trek back to the orphanage. Later, she'd ask Micah what Salvador meant when he said Micah was responsible for the death of his family.

Twenty minutes later, they arrived at Lake Tomalis without further incident and she had no trouble spotting the red pole and green flag Maria had told her to look for. Now she just had to find the clearing.

When the canoe scraped the muddy bottom, Amy was the first to climb out, ignoring the pain from her bites. Micah and

Jonathas followed, with Jonathas pulling the craft up to beach it on the shore. How they were going to fit two more people in it for the return trip, she had no idea. Right now, she just wanted to concentrate on getting to the right place.

A path to the right of where they'd landed led into the jungle. Amy winced at the thought of another hike, but didn't say anything. Micah asked, "Where are you supposed to meet?"

"She said 'the clearing near Lake Tomalis.' I'm guessing that path leads to it. Maria didn't seem to think I'd have any trouble finding it."

"Let me lead. Jonathas, why don't bring up the rear? That way if there's trouble, we can do our best to keep Amy out of it."

Amy's heart clenched. He would protect her with his life. The knowledge nearly sent her to her knees. And she didn't think he'd do it just because he was a SEAL. Obviously he had feelings for her; otherwise, he'd have gotten on that plane and disappeared from her life.

He'd missed his flight to come find her. *Thank You, Jesus.*

"Micah, what are you doing here?"

Her soft question brought him to her side. He crooked his finger and ran it down her cheek. His hooded blue eyes stared at her, as though he were trying to figure out whether to answer her. Finally he said, "We'll talk about it tomorrow on the flight home."

So he was coming with her. In spite of the pain from her wounds, a smile tugged her lips. "Okay."

"In fact, we have a lot to talk about. But right now, we need to get going. Keep your eyes open, all right?"

"Right."

The threesome headed down the path, creeping along slowly, and Micah holding his gun ready. Tension zipped through Amy. She felt excited about talking to Micah tomorrow, all the while praying that they would live to have the conversation. Focusing on the task before her, she stepped in Micah's footprints, hearing Jonathas's reassuring presence behind her.

Five short minutes later, they stepped to the edge of the clearing Maria must have been talking about. Micah held a finger to his lips, motioning Amy to come up next to him. She stepped beside him. He placed a hand on her shoulder and then leaned down to whisper in her ear, "We're on time. Do you see anything?"

Amy shook her head.

"So, what are you supposed to do now?"

"Wait, I guess," she whispered back.

Her gaze scanned the small open area, taking in the sights, sounds and smells around her. If she weren't so jumpy, she might have enjoyed the impromptu jungle tour. It was a fascinating place. But she was here for another reason.

She pushed a branch away from her face, wincing as the action pulled at the bites on her arm. Her leg throbbed; the cut on her stomach zinged pain every time she moved. She ignored it all.

Bushes fifty feet to their left shivered, rustled, then were parted. Micah drew her back slightly, one hand cupped around her elbow, the other curled around the butt of his gun. Amy drew comfort from his presence as two figures stepped out. Amy recognized Maria and assumed the young girl at her side was Lucia.

"That's them."

Amy sidled in front of Micah, venturing closer to the two women. Maria held a rifle in her left hand. Which made sense. Of course she wouldn't travel through the jungle without a weapon. "Hello, Maria." No way was she calling the woman grandmother. "Lucia, I'm your cousin, Amy."

Lucia took a step closer to her grandmother, but smiled a tentative, scared smile at Amy's greeting. Maria nodded. Glancing over her shoulder, she gave the girl a gentle shove in Amy's direction. "Go."

With tears trembling on her midnight-colored lashes, Lucia moved as ordered. Yet Amy thought she detected a glimmer of excitement in the girl's eyes. Maria must have explained to Lucia that she would be going to America with Amy.

Cajoling, Amy begged Maria, "Please come with us, turn yourself in and work with the authorities. Tell them where the camp is. They can rescue the other children there and may offer leniency if you do." Amy moved toward Maria, taking her hand, hoping Maria wouldn't resist her efforts.

"No. My life is almost over. But this one deserves better. I need to do at least one right thing in my life. This is it. Take care of her."

"But if you go back, they'll kill you if they find out what you've done. Lucia won't be safe as long as they exist. Turn them in."

Maria shrugged. "It will all work out. You have Lucia. You will take her to America where she will be safe. Here are her papers." Amy took the small plastic-wrapped package. Dirt covered it, as if it had been buried and just recently dug up.

"Now go. I am dying anyway. The cancer. So, now it's time."

But she would die without Christ. *Jesus, please, what do I say?* "Maria, please. I want the chance to get to know you, to talk to you. And . . . and don't you want to see your daughter, Juanita, one more time?"

At this question, Maria paused, closing her eyes briefly. When she opened them, there was nothing left but hardness. "No, it is too late for that."

"Then let me pray with you." Amy was desperate. She had to find the location of the camp.

"Pray with me?" Maria gave a phlegmy, humorless chuckle that turned into a hacking cough. "I do not think your prayers will help too much."

Amy stepped closer. "Please?"

Shrugging, Maria acquiesced. Amy said a short, heartfelt prayer, asking for protection for Maria and for her to come to know Him personally. Frantically, she tried to figure out how to convince the woman to stay with her. Unfortunately, nothing came to mind. When she said, "Amen," Maria squeezed her hand, hugged Lucia . . . then raised her rifle to point it at Micah.

Amy gasped.

The rifle cracked.
And Micah hit the jungle floor.

FOURTEEN

"Micah!"

He heard her scream, felt the thud of something land across his back. When Maria had lifted the rifle in his direction, instinct had sent him to the ground. Now he rolled to his knees in one smooth motion, his hand grabbing for the gun he'd stuck in his waistband. By the time he had the pistol up, Maria was disappearing through the trees.

"Micah?" Amy's voice came to him while he was considering giving chase.

"I warned you," he exploded. "What was that crazy woman doing?" He turned to Amy, ready to blast her for trusting so easily when his gaze followed hers. To the headless snake still twitching on the ground beside him.

Slowly, Amy's eyes rose from the snake to him. "Saving your life, I think."

Micah shook his head and muttered,

"What is it with snakes? If I never see another one again . . ."

"Are we ready to go, *senhor?*" Jonathas asked.

"Please, let's get out of here. We still need to take care of Salvador."

Amy had a grip on Lucia's small hand. "She's got her papers. The plane tickets are all back at the orphanage. Since I didn't get the location of the rebel camp, we'll have to get out of here and back to the U.S. as quickly as possible. Once they realize Maria betrayed them, they'll come after Lucia. Can the four of us fit in that canoe?"

Micah ran a hand through is already tousled hair. "We'll have to."

They made their way back through the jungle, guided by the large flashlight Jonathas had thought to bring. Micah sent up a prayer of thanks for that. Amy's flashlight was with Salvador.

A sigh of relief escaped Micah as they came to the canoe, still on the beach. The way things had been going lately, Micah really hadn't expected it to be there. He directed the three into the vessel.

Fortunately, it was a rather large canoe and the four of them were able to squeeze in without sinking the thing, though it rode dangerously low in the water. Micah shook his head. "Amy, you and Lucia stay as still as possible. Jonathas and I'll row."

Micah picked up the paddle, and Jonathas followed his lead.

"Here, Amy, hold this light so we can see where we're going. The last thing we need is to run into some stray debris." Micah handed her the light and Amy did as requested. Together, Micah and Jonathas made pretty good time, although they were rowing against the current.

As he rhythmically pulled the paddle, he studied her bent head. What was he going to do with her? He truly loved the stubborn woman, but did he love her enough to get past his anger with her mother? He sure hoped so because he wasn't willing to walk out of her life again.

Two hours later, they arrived at the spot where they'd originally boarded the canoe. The extra time they took to come back was from rowing against the current. Leaving the canoe on the beach where they'd found it, the group wearily retraced their earlier path through the jungle. In another few days, no one would know there'd been a path made.

Micah breathed a sigh when the orphanage came into view. More lights than usual burned throughout the building, indicating abnormal activity.

"I guess Salvador made it back," Amy said.

"Let's hope the chief was here to manage his arrival," Micah muttered, hoping to get his hands on the kid before he was shipped off to the nearest jail.

Amy suddenly thought to ask, "Why would he blame you for the death of his family?"

Micah blinked. "What? I have no idea. I didn't have anything to do with his family. I've never even seen the kid before he arrived at the orphanage." Micah stared down into her sparkling blue eyes, which were illuminated by the glow of the moon breaking through the canopy of leaves.

"All I know is he says that's the reason he tried to kill you. You killed his family, he tried to kill you. When that failed, he decided to get rid of me — so you would suffer like he did."

Shivers rushed through Micah, causing him to shake and sweat at the same time. He had absolutely no clue as to why Salvador believed he had anything to do with his family's death, but he was going to find out. Right now.

When Amy rushed into the lobby, the first thing she saw was Carlita sitting in Salvador's lap. The second thing her eyes landed on was the chief of police, David Ruibero standing beside the siblings. Salvador's hands were bound behind him, the look in his eyes one of defiance mixed with defeat.

Lucia stood right inside the door, eyes wide, taking it all in. Amy shot her a pleading look, trying to convey the fact that she needed to deal with this situation. The girl gave a tentative smile, indicating she understood. Breathing a sigh of relief, Amy turned back to Salvador. The door swooshed behind her. She assumed that was Micah and Jonathas making their entrance.

"Oh, Salvador," she breathed standing in front of him. "How could you?"

Hate oozed from him, his glare intense enough to make her flinch. "How could I? Easy," he spat, looking up at Micah, who stood behind her. Eyes focused on the man he'd targeted, he declared, "You killed my family. Now you want to take the only one I have left. I couldn't allow it."

Micah moved forward, frowning in puzzlement. "How did I kill your family? When did this happen?"

"I worked for Cruz."

Jonathas exploded. "I knew you did. I couldn't prove it, but I thought you looked familiar so I kept watching you, waiting,

268

trying to figure out your plans. But Carlita . . . you love her so much, I didn't put it together until just now."

Eyes on Jonathas, Salvador said, "Your father blamed me for helping the woman escape with the little boy, Mattie. He sent four men to kill my family." He turned his attention from Jonathas back to Micah. "Cruz's wife, she asked me to help her get away from her husband and she would pay me much money. I helped her and the boy get away. But Cruz found out and sent in men to kill my family. You were one of those men."

Micah sputtered, "No way. I don't even know what you're talking about."

Carlita shifted, popped her thumb in her mouth and leaned her head on Salvador's shoulder. Amy swallowed the lump in her throat. *Oh, Father, help me.*

A vein throbbed in the young man's neck as he seethed. "They meant so little to you. You kill and don't remember. I heard the orders for the assignment, I just didn't realize Cruz meant my family." He choked on his grief, the pain of his loss too great. Gaining control, he started at Micah. Amy wondered where the breakdown in communication had occurred. Micah would never have been involved in the killing of innocents; he would have blown his cover first.

Tears of rage, grief and hate slid silently down Salvador's cheeks. Bowing his head, he said through clenched teeth, "I promised my parents I would watch after her. I stood over their bodies and promised. My older sister, Natalia, is somewhere out there, sold into slavery. I have nightmares about what she is going through and I can't help her. I thought I could help Carlita, and at the same time kill the ones responsible for my family's deaths."

Micah suddenly realized the "assignment" Salvador referred to. He'd been deep under-cover observing, watching Cruz. He remembered the day he'd been puzzled by the man's extreme agitation, wondering what was going on with him. Finally, Cruz had called a meeting and told the four men gathered in his office that he had a special assignment for them.

Money exchanged hands. Information was given out on a need-to-know basis. The man placed in charge of the assignment would give the orders. Micah had never found out what those orders were as Cruz changed his mind about Micah's role in his organization.

Exasperated, Micah raked a hand through his sweaty hair. "I wasn't on that assignment. I was told it was cancelled and I was to cover the boy that had just arrived." Micah felt as though he'd been sucker punched. His gut actually ached as he realized Cruz had moved him because he'd found out about Micah from Amy's mother — and had planned for him to die along with the little boy. If Micah had known the details about that assignment — and not been told it was cancelled — he might have been able to save Salvador's family.

Just more deaths Amy's mother could be held responsible for. He swallowed. No way would he ever let her know that. He continued, "As it was, I was doing my best to get word to another SEAL team that Cruz was at the mansion and they needed to hurry up and organize a time to raid the place. But I promise, Salvador, I was never there."

At first, Salvador looked as if he didn't believe Micah, then his shoulders slumped in defeat. "I will go to jail now." He swallowed hard, looked up at Amy. "I have no right to ask, but will you please take care of Carlita? Go ahead and take her to the U.S." He shuddered. "I have no way to earn the money she needs, no way to keep my promise to my dead parents. The only way I can help her now is to let her go. With you."

Anger, hurt, pity. Micah couldn't decide which emotion took priority. He did feel grateful that God had watched over him and Amy all this time.

"Micah?"

The female voice brought all heads around to stare at the immaculately dressed red-headed woman standing in the door's entrance.

Micah blinked. "Mom?"

He had to be hallucinating. He blinked again, but her image was still there. A petite slender woman with beautiful auburn hair pulled up in a stylish clip. Tears mingled with the mascara that ran down her cheeks to drip off her chin. "Mom?" he breathed again.

Christina McKnight sobbed, nodded once and ran into his arms. Micah folded them around her, breathed in the scent he remembered from childhood, a mixture of roses and mint tea.

"You remember? But Amy said —"

"It all came back a few days ago."

"Oh, Micah, I thought we'd never see you again. I'd finally given up hope you were alive and . . . it's an answer to my prayers." She pulled back, ran her hands down his face, over his scars.

272

"How'd you get here? Where's Dad? Cassidy?"

No sooner were the words out of his mouth than the people in question were coming through the door, followed by two men Micah knew were his father's bodyguards.

"Micah!" Cassidy's squeal singed him. He turned just in time to catch her as she hurled herself into his now-empty arms. "Micah, I can't believe it's true. When Amy called and told us you were alive, I just . . . I couldn't . . . Oh, God is so good, isn't He? Has your memory come back?"

He nodded against the side of her curly red head. She gave him another neck-crushing squeeze.

The phone rang, and he vaguely registered Anna leaving to answer it. Amy stood next to Salvador, watching the family reunion. He looked up at the tall man who now had an arm around Micah's mother and a wide-eyed little blond-headed girl in the crook of his other arm.

"Hi, Dad."

Jonathan McKnight swallowed hard. His lips trembled. "My son."

Micah untangled himself from Cassidy, pressed a kiss to her forehead, then embraced his father. His mother took the child, giving Jonathan both arms with which to hold Micah. Father and son clung, weeping together unashamedly. Micah felt another hand on his shoulder, turned to see Gabriel Sinclair, his best friend, standing there with tears leaking down his cheeks.

Dark brown eyes silently asked if Micah held a grudge. Gabe had practically forced Micah into the mission that had nearly killed him and had cost him more than two years of his life. Micah had resisted the mission Gabe had ordered.

Micah studied the man in front of him. He had no hard feelings. Gabe had done his job the way he'd been trained — to the best of his ability. Micah couldn't hold that against him. In fact, Gabe had his utmost respect.

Hesitantly, Gabe held out a hand, obviously expecting Micah to reject him. Micah pulled him into a bear hug, then pushed him back. "What are you doing here?"

"I . . . uh . . . Amy hasn't told you?"

Micah frowned. "Told me what?"

"I sorta married your sister." Gabe shot Micah a sheepish grin. Cassidy giggled like the newlywed she was.

"You what?" Micah yelled. He looked at his father. "And you allowed this?"

Jonathan's eyes went wide. "You think you

could have stopped her?"

Grumbling good-naturedly, Micah muttered, "You have a point."

Amy's giggle broke the tension. She rushed to Cassidy throwing her arms around her best friend. "I'm so glad you're okay. Was the hurricane bad?"

"Bad enough. The boat rocked for quite a while before we were able to dock. We were all a bunch of sick people." Cassidy grimaced. "Not a pretty sight, that's for sure."

"All right, folks, I'm just as thrilled as anyone when we have a happy ending, but I've got some legal issues to take care of here, and I'd like to do it before I have to drive back in the rain," the police chief said. Thunder sounded in the distance. The chief's voice brought everyone back to the present situation.

"Carlita? Carlita? Where are you?" Salvador stood, hands still bound behind his back.

Amy looked at Jonathas. "Did you see her leave?"

He shook his head. "No, I was watching all the commotion."

Jonathas volunteered, "Let me check her room. She may have gotten tired and decided to go lie down." He left and Anna walked back into the room, her face white.

Amy rushed to her. "What is it?"

"They raided the camp already."

"What? How? We've only been gone from Lake Tomalis for a couple of hours and I never got the location."

"Apparently, the authorities got an anonymous tip *before* you guys even got to Lake Tomalis. They put together a sting operation that included a team of Army Rangers they had on standby for this very thing. They called me because they want to bring the children that survived the raid here to the orphanage. Several of the higher-ranking rebels survived and are in custody — including your policeman attacker, Roberto."

Amy shot a glance at Lucia, making sure the girl wasn't listening. She was talking softly to Alexis. "My grandmother?"

"No word yet," Anna said. "I know the camp moves a lot, so there's no telling whether she was there or not. I know you thought she and Lucia walked a long way, but it's possible the camp was closer than you believed. I honestly think it was Maria who tipped the authorities off before meeting you. It's the only way they would have known how to find the camp. Once she had Lucia out of there, she knew there'd be no going back."

Amy drew in a long breath. Maria had

done this on purpose. She was dying and this was her way of doing something good with her life. Allowing Lucia to escape from the camp had signed her death warrant. "She gave up the camp to get Lucia out. If any of those rebels escaped the raid, they may come here to exact their revenge." Maria had sacrificed herself for her granddaughter.

"I can't find her!"

Jonathas's shout brought all attention to him. His brown eyes were wide, worry stamped on his young features. He might not like Carlita's brother, but he had always treated the little girl with nothing but love and respect.

Amy frowned, "Did you check the playroom?"

"Yes, I've checked everywhere. She's not in this building."

"Where else would she go?" This was definitely odd behavior for the little girl. She worshipped her big brother and kept him in sight whenever possible. Salvador sat in the chair, hands still bound, worry written across his face. Shifting, he looked at Amy and answered her question. "I don't know, but you've got to find her. There's a storm coming and you know how she hates the thunder."

Amy nodded.

Micah took over. "All right, everyone, spread out. We need to find that little girl before the storm hits."

"I'll go this way," Gabe immediately offered. He looked at Micah's father. "Sir, you want to help?"

"Of course. Tell me what I need to do."

While Micah and Gabe formulated the plan, Cassidy said, "I'll stay with the girls." She nodded toward Alexis and Lucia. The chief put in a call for a unit to be dispatched to the orphanage.

Amy stopped to grab the flashlight from her pack, then ran out the lobby doors. "Carlita!" she called into the darkness, desperately trying to hear over the night sounds of the jungle.

Thunder rumbled in the distance. Soon it would be overhead, and Carlita would be one scared little girl. Amy glanced at the jungle. Surely she wouldn't dare try to head into the thickness.

"Wait! Come back!" The shout came from Salvador still inside. Amy hurried back in. "What is it? You know her best, Sal. What would she be thinking?"

"That she doesn't want to be separated from me."

Gabe called out, "Micah told me about

the chapel. I'll check there." He trotted off into the woods toward the little chapel Amy and Maria had used as their rendezvous place only a few short days ago.

Think, Amy, think.

Could someone from the rebel camp have followed her back here after her meeting with Maria? Would they have snatched Carlita as revenge for Maria bringing Lucia to Amy?

It just didn't seem possible.

Lightning split the sky, turning night into day, flooding the lobby with its brightness. Amy blinked against it. Her heart clenched at the fear Carlita must be feeling. *Please, Jesus, be with that little girl. Keep her safe. Don't let tragedy strike now.* So many dangers lurked in the jungle, dangers that could kill a small child so quickly. She shuddered and pushed the scary thoughts aside as she focused on searching for Carlita.

Micah came back in. "He think of anything?"

"Nothing." She bit her lip thinking, racking her brain to figure out what the child might be thinking. "I don't see her going into the jungle. She'd be too scared. Unfortunately, I can't think of where she *would* go."

"She'd hide. Somewhere where Salvador

would be able to find her."

Micah looked over at the boy who sat with his shoulders hunched against his bonds, eyes ping-ponging back and forth between Amy and him.

Swallowing hard, Salvador focused on Amy. "I don't know. I cannot even think. She is nowhere inside, but she hates storms so there is no way she would go outside."

"Would she go on the river?" Amy asked, dreading to hear the answer. "She left before the storm started sounding this bad."

Salvador paled. "No," he whispered under his breath. "She wouldn't, would she?"

He whirled around to face the chief. "Let me go to the river, please. I won't escape. I couldn't go far if I did. I just need to see . . ."

The chief hesitated. Amy pleaded, "Please, she's only six years old. If he can help . . ."

Finally, the chief nodded, but warned, "Go, but I'm right behind you — and I'm not taking the cuffs off."

Before she or Micah could respond, the young man jumped up from his chair and took off toward the dock on the river. The chief, Amy and Micah followed at a fast clip, praying the little girl wasn't out on the rocking water. The small canoe could easily overturn in the surges caused by the wind.

The four of them came to the dock, and

Amy caught her breath as her nightmare materialized before her eyes. A lone canoe floated about fifty yards from shore, over-turned and definitely empty. An object near the edge of the river caught her eye as it was tossed to and fro by the increasing violence of the waves. Salvador saw it, too, raced down to the edge of the river and stared down at it. Then he let out a wail that raised goose bumps on Amy's flesh.

He sank to his knees in the mud, crying, "Carlita, my little sister. Come back." Drop-ping face-first into Carlita's favorite toy, her bunny, he wailed in heart-wrenching agony. Amy frantically ran her gaze over the water, but if Carlita was somewhere in its depths, it was too late to help her now. Tears dripped down her cheeks. Micah put an arm around her, pulling her into his shoulder. She let him offer the comfort for a brief mo-ment, then pulled away.

She went to Salvador who, with his arms awkwardly behind his back, rocked and weaved with his grief. Disregarding the mud, Amy sank to her knees beside him. She let him howl his misery as she picked up the filthy bunny. The chief stood watch-ing, knowing he could catch the agony-stricken brother at any time if he had to.

Leaning back, Salvador clenched his teeth

and said, "I told her if there was ever trouble at the orphanage to get the canoe, get in it to hide and I would know to find her on the water."

Her heart breaking, Amy wanted to cry out her own sorrow. *Oh, God, why did you allow this? Please, Jesus, make this right. I don't even know what to pray, God, but do something, please.*

They'd have to call the authorities to drag the river, but most likely the body of the little girl would never be found. Amy felt a hand under her elbow. Looking up, she stared into Micah's wet blue eyes. He'd cared for Carlita, too. He helped Amy up, then pulled Salvador to his shaky feet. Together, the three made their way back to the orphanage where Gabe, Micah's family, two other police officers and Anna met them with questions in their eyes. Salvador wrenched himself away, still sobbing. The chief walked with him allowing him time to work out his grief.

Flatly, Micah stated, "We think she went out on the river. Her bunny was floating out near the shore and the canoe was out on the river . . . upside down. Carlita never went anywhere without that bunny. She loved it."

Grief choking her, Amy whirled to run, to

get away and have a good cry, when move-ment captured her attention. She gasped. "What was that?"

Micah looked at her as if she were crazy. "What?"

"I saw something. Over there. Carlita hated storms. I think she may have tried to get in the canoe to go out on the river, but what if she got scared when the thunder and lightning started? She would find another place Salvador would be sure to find her . . . and she'd want to be inside," Amy stated, excitement and hope coloring her voice.

Micah stared at her, confusion written on his features. "But she's not inside. We've searched everywhere."

Amy walked toward the cars parked in the mud near the entrance to the lobby. The wind whipped her hair around her eyes, and she pushed it back. Thunder boomed closer, and a fat raindrop hit her square on the nose as she looked in the first car, then the second. When she came to the third, the chief's car, she pulled open the door.

Carlita sat upright in the backseat where she stirred in her sleep with the next crash of thunder. Joy flooded Amy. *Oh, thank You, precious Jesus, thank You.*

"She must have moved her head from side to side and I was standing at just the right angle to see it. That's the movement I saw."

Amy reached in gently to shake the sleeping child. "Carlita, sweetie, wake up."

Carlita opened her big brown eyes. Amy reached in to pull her out of the car. The child resisted, frowning and shaking her head. Amy stopped. "What's wrong, baby? You gave us all a scare. We thought you were out on the river."

Another negative shake of her little dark head.

"Salvador. Come on, honey, we have to go see Salvador. He thinks . . . Well, never mind what he thinks. Come on."

Still frowning, Carlita allowed herself to be dragged from the vehicle. More rain started to fall and she pressed into Amy. Picking up the girl, Amy headed for the doors of the orphanage when she heard a shout.

"Hey!"

It was Gabe.

"That boy is going into the river!"

FIFTEEN

Micah heard Gabe's warning through the roar in his ears. Carlita was alive; Salvador thought she was dead in the churning water.

Turning, Micah raced for the river. Pounding down the dock, he stopped at the end. Salvador was swimming for the canoe . . . his only illumination the moon shining its full glory. "Salvador, come back!"

The boy kept swimming. Amy charged up beside Micah, two heavy flashlights in hand. The chief, clutching his forehead, blood oozing between his fingers, arrived with Gabe, who had Carlita clutched in his arms.

The chief huffed, "I let him out of his cuffs. I felt sorry for him with his sister and all. He was a mess and said he wanted to clean himself up. When I stepped back, he came around with something and caught me in the head. It stunned me long enough to allow him to get away."

Micah grabbed one of the lights and

pointed it out on the water scanning the surface. Caimans were nocturnal animals, known to sleep during the day and hunt at night. Salvador's splashing would only bring attention to himself. And with the churning water . . .

"Salvador, Carlita's alive!" he called. "Come back!"

It seemed to take forever, but Salvador finally managed to reach the overturned canoe. Treading water, struggling with the weight, he flipped it upright. Of course it was empty; he just didn't realize the person he was looking for was on the dock. Micah watched him lean his forehead against the wood, his shoulders shaking with the force of his sobs.

"Salvador!" The small sweet voice beside him brought his attention to the little girl in Gabe's arms. Carlita had spoken.

Amy stared in shock, then a wide grin split her lips. She glanced at Micah to share the moment of joy, and Micah reveled being there with her, hearing Carlita speak for the first time since her parents' deaths.

"Call him again, sweetheart. It's hard to hear over the wind."

"Salvador!"

Salvador heard her. His head shot up, and he looked toward the sound, but there was

286

no way for him to be able to see anything except the bright spotlight glaring back at him from the dock.

Thinking fast, Amy turned the light on Carlita, who waved to her brother. "Come back, Salvador! I'm here."

Salvador seemed to be in shock, unable to move. A wave swept him under, and he came up sputtering. Micah wondered if he should grab one of the boats and motor out to get the boy.

Amy hollered, "Swim!"

Salvador swam with strong strokes, fighting against the current to get back to the sister he loved. He reached the shore of the river safely. Panting, gasping, Salvador squinted through the now falling rain.

Gabe passed Carlita to Micah, who hurried to the end of the dock. The reunion between the siblings brought almost as much joy to his heart as the moment when he'd turned to see his mother's face only moments ago. And a deep sadness, too, because Salvador's actions would have consequences that would separate brother and sister for a very long time.

Still crying, Salvador swept his sister into his arms and hugged her. She wrapped her little arms around his neck and squeezed back, giggling now that Salvador had her.

She cupped his face in her little hands. "Salvador, you came back."

"And you're alive!"

"I was afraid when the policeman came," Carlita said. "I remember what you said about if there was trouble. I went to get in the canoe but it got away from me. And I dropped my bunny in the water. And then I was so tired, but I didn't want to go back in where the policeman was because he was going to take you away. So I got in his car. If he was taking you to jail, I was going, too."

Thunder cracked again and lightning followed quick on its heels. "Come on," Micah said, "let's get inside and get dried off. We need to let everyone know we found her."

The group trudged back to the orphanage, dripping with water, their happiness marred by the realization that Salvador would have to face the consequences of his actions. The chief had a tight grip on his arm. Micah took the little girl from Salvador who stood meekly, allowing the chief to cuff him once more. Micah passed Carlita off to Gabe, then snagged Amy's hand. He held it until they reached the door. While everyone else was entering, he pulled her back.

She looked up at him. "Micah?"

"I don't have much time, so I'm going to

make this quick. Come with me to the chapel."

"Now?"

"Now."

"But what about your family, all those people —"

He placed a finger over her lips. "Please?"

She nodded. "Okay. Anna will be busy helping everyone settle in their rooms for the night. We probably have a few minutes."

"Exactly." He pulled her with him in the drenching rain down the path to the little stone chapel. Pushing open the door, he stepped inside and she followed, shivering in the damp coolness.

"I'm fr-freezing," Amy stuttered through chattering teeth. "Th-there's a bathroom with a linen closet next to the door behind the baptism pool. Let's see if there are some towels, okay?"

Micah felt chill bumps popping up on his arms. "That sounds good. Sit here and I'll find us something."

He helped Amy into the pew, then went to find the towels. Two minutes later, he was back. "Here, wrap up in this."

Shivering, she reached up for the towel. He helped her place it around her shoulders as he tried to decide what words to say. Scooting into the pew next to her, he felt her warmth as he wrapped his arms around her and pulled her to him. She didn't resist, so he took that as a good sign. Resting his chin on her head, he said, "I love you, Amy."

She sighed. "I know. I love you, too."

"So, what do we do now?"

Amy flinched at the question, wanting to ignore it, but forced to face it. "I guess the big question is, can you forgive me for being who I am?"

"I love who you are. I hate who your mother is."

"I can't say I'm exactly thrilled with that one myself. Unfortunately, I can't change it."

"No, you can't. I can't, either. I also can't see letting her ruin what we have."

Amy gave a dry laugh. "Well, if you want to do her in for good, just tell her we're . . ." She sighed. "Never mind. I shouldn't make light of the situation. I've prayed and prayed about this, Micah. I'll be honest with you. I want everything we could have together. And if I have to say goodbye to you again, I think it will actually —" she stopped to swallow back the tears that threatened to fall "— literally break my heart. But I want what God wants."

"Yeah," he breathed. "Me, too."

"So again, I guess it all boils down to whether or not you can forgive me for being the daughter of the woman who tried to kill you."

"I think I'm going to have to disagree with you on that one."

"Really?"

"I don't think I have to forgive you for being your mother's daughter; I think *we,* as in you and me, have to forgive your mother. Period."

"Don't you think I've tried?" she cried, pulling back to stare into his electric blue-gray eyes. How had she not recognized him the moment he'd opened them weeks ago? She focused on his words.

"Yeah, I think you've tried. But we can't do it under our own power. That's going to have to come from God. I've been a Christian a long time, Amy, but I've only come to realize recently that the God I accepted as a teenager wants a personal, intimate relationship with me. He's not up there waiting for me to dial the spiritual 9-1-1 line. He's there all the time, wanting to hear from me on a daily basis. You helped me realize that, too. And I think we're going to have to make that choice to forgive if we're going to have any kind of future together."

"I'm glad, so very glad that you've grown

closer to God, but there's nothing about my mother that makes me *want* to offer her forgiveness. She doesn't deserve it or *want* it, either."

"But from everything I've ever read, heard or studied about God, none of us deserve it — His forgiveness, that is. And He forgave us before we even realized we needed it — or wanted it. That's what the cross did."

Something she'd known, of course, and she also knew she didn't deserve God's grace of forgiveness, but had accepted it willingly when presented with the truth of His love. A new understanding was sinking in as they talked it out. "That's true. God offers it to each and every one of us. Undeserving, repentant or not, he still *offers* it. It's there for the taking."

"So, I guess we should try to do the same, shouldn't we?"

"Do you know how hard that will be?"

"You have to ask?"

She blew out a sigh. "I guess not. But she's so hard, Micah. She doesn't even want forgiveness. She's not interested in Christ's love. There's not a remorseful bone in her body, just evil."

"And yet, Christ died for her, too."

"Yes, He did." Amy fiddled with the edge of the towel as she thought about it.

"So, it seems to me we should think about making the conscious decision to forgive your mother . . . even if our hearts aren't ready to do it yet. Hopefully, one day they will be. Think about it. All she's ever known has been Satan's lies. Maybe it's time someone presented her with God's truth."

"We could work on it, I suppose." She sighed. Just thinking about it made her wince, and yet she knew it was something she was going to have to do. With God's help.

"I'm not saying it'll happen overnight, but I'm willing to try if you are. I want to spend the rest of my life spreading the truth of God's love to anyone and everyone who'll listen."

A thought struck her. She whispered, "The belt of truth."

"What?"

She smiled quoting, "Ephesians 6:14. 'Stand firm then, with the belt of truth buckled around your waist.' " Amy reached out to lay a quivering hand on his waist where his birthmark lay underneath his shirt. "You've always had it. You think God may have been preparing you for this moment? That these were the plans He had for you when He formed you?"

Micah stretched out his left hand, examined the scars crisscrossing the back of it, traveling up to disappear under his sleeve. "Maybe." He dropped his hand to cover hers. "I never thought of the birthmark in that context. A belt of truth." He laughed, sobered and said, "I think perhaps God has decided to take what was meant for evil and turned it for good. For His glory. I want to rescue more children, Amy. I can't stand what's going on here."

"But how can we ever rescue enough?"

"One at a time, with God's help and leading. Just like with Carlita and Lucia. And Natalia. I'm going to do my best to find her."

Amy looked deep into his bottomless blue eyes. "Do you think that if I could forgive my mother, I'd finally have the peace I've been searching for? I mean, just knowing God gives me more peace than I ever thought possible, but I mean the peace that comes from forgiveness . . . true forgiveness."

"I think it's a start . . . and I think that's all God asks of us — just to have a willing heart. He'll do the rest." Squeezing her close, he pressed a kiss to the top of her head.

She snuggled close, enjoying the freedom of being able to be close to Micah, and sighed. "Okay, I can have a willing heart — I think. The rest will definitely have to be up to Him, though."

"Sounds like a plan. Do you think you would be willing to marry me so we can adopt a couple of those kids in there and get them the help they need?" His voice sounded rough, as though the emotions clamoring through him were struggling to break out.

Amy searched his face again, seeing the love for her and the fierce need to do something to help those who couldn't help themselves expressed so openly in his eyes. Still, she had to ask, "Are you sure you're ready for a ready-made family?"

Without a shadow of a doubt, he said, "I am if you are."

"I am," she declared, the knot in her throat threatening to choke off her words. She just couldn't believe everything that happened had brought them to this point. It could only be God. And she silently thanked Him for His goodness, for not letting her stubbornness and sometimes do-it-herself attitude get in the way of His plan for her life. And Micah's.

"Uh-uh —" He bent closer, hovering his lips a hair's breath away from hers. She closed her eyes, breathing in the spicy tang of aftershave that still lingered, mingled with sweat and the scent that belonged just to him. "Wrong answer."

"Huh?" Her eyes popped open in confusion and she wondered if being close to him like this would always turn her brain to mush. Probably.

He grinned at her. "It's not, 'I am' . . . it's, 'I do.' "

"Oh, okay, I do, too." She giggled, then sighed as his lips settled ever so sweetly over hers to seal the deal.

EPILOGUE

Six months later
Landrum, South Carolina
The back door slammed.

"Mama, Oliver hit me with a water balloon!" Carlita stepped into the kitchen, disgust and water dripping from her. Amy bit the inside of her lip to keep from laughing. "Go into the bathroom and dry off. I'll go fuss at Oliver."

She stepped outside onto the porch to see Oliver, their next-door neighbor who treated Carlita like a little sister, and two friends from church sitting in the grass, taking turns throwing water balloons at a makeshift target.

"Oliver!" Amy called from her spot on the porch.

The teen looked up. Guilt flashed across his features. "Yes, ma'am?"

"What did Carlita do to make you toss a water balloon at her?"

A relieved grin stretched his lips across his tanned face. "She was teasing me about a girl I like at church." Concern flickered briefly. "She's not upset, is she?"

"No, she's fine. Disgusted, but the way a younger sister should be with an older brother." Like the older brother she missed. Salvador was now serving time in a Brazilian jail.

His shoulders relaxed. "Well, good, because she deserved it."

Amy gave a silent laugh and went back inside. Carlita skipped out of the bathroom, a smile on her sweet face, the incident clearly forgotten. "When's Daddy coming home?"

"Soon, I hope."

Carlita ran off and Amy glanced at the phone. *Come on, Micah. Call me.*

She'd survived calling her mother. And to her surprise, found her hate fading to something that resembled sadness with each prayer she said. Someone once said it was hard to hate someone you prayed for. Amy was finding this to be true.

Micah often went to the jail and tried to visit. The woman never would consent to see him, but he went once a week, carrying her items, a Bible, notes from a sermon, whatever he felt led to do. He confessed it was one of the hardest things he'd ever done, but God was working in his heart also.

As he worked to rescue the children, he'd seen little ones, youngsters, toddlers, teenagers, just like Juanita had once been, living in rebel camps, on the streets, with no chances in life but an early death. He said once he'd seen that, it had been a little easier to let go of the anger toward Juanita.

Thirty minutes later, Amy heard the door slam. "Anyone home?" Micah's voice pulled her into the foyer.

"Daddy!" Carlita squealed hurling herself in Micah's arms.

Amy had been waiting for Micah's call all day. Now he was here. She caught his eye with a silent question. His answering smile sent shivers up her spine. They'd been married six months now, neither of them wanting to put off the event they knew in their hearts would take place eventually.

Now Micah and Amy were a family of four living in a rambling Victorian mansion with forty-two acres of land right outside the growing town of Landrum, South Carolina.

"Well?" she whispered.

He nodded pulling her to him for a kiss. "Did you make your phone call?"

"Yes, and I'll tell you about it later. Now . . . when?" she persisted.

"Soon."

The sound of a car pulling up outside pulled her from her thoughts. "Is that her?"

Micah smiled mysteriously. "Let's find out."

Lucia joined them as they stepped back outside to see who would exit the car driven by Gabe. A young lady of about twenty-four years old climbed from the backseat, taking in her surroundings with an expression of awe.

Micah whispered to the little girl, "That's your sister, Natalia." They'd talked to Carlita at length about the young woman who might be able to come live with them one day, talked about her so much Carlita felt as if she knew her.

"Natalia!" she cried.

"Carlita," Natalia breathed. She put her hand to her mouth, and blinked as though afraid she might be dreaming and wake up any second. Then it was all action. She ran to throw her arms around the little girl.

Amy gripped Micah's hand. "You did it."

"Wasn't easy."

Shortly after their marriage, he'd returned to Brazil to specifically hunt for Natalia Orozco. By interviewing each person captured from Lucia's camp, Micah had finally come across one of the men who'd been

300

involved in the killing of Salvador and Carlita's parents.

With promises of a lighter sentence for any information, the man had given them the location of Natalia. Weeks of work resulted in a well-organized raid involving SEALs and Rangers that had led to the capture of more human-trafficking criminals and the rescue of several hundred victims — including Natalia.

Natalia picked up Carlita to kiss her on the cheek.

Amy whispered, "God's certainly blessed us beyond anything I could have ever imagined."

"Are you sure you're okay with me returning to work that's dangerous? Rescuing these children and other victims of human trafficking. You know what it entails."

She sighed. "I can't promise not to worry when you're gone, but if this is what God has called you to do, I'll deal with it, with His help — but thanks for asking."

He squeezed her close for a moment. "I've got a lot to live for. I won't take any unnecessary chances."

"I know, Micah."

He looked back over at the siblings. Lucia chatted away with them, seeming to be comfortable in the midst of the circle

"Three kids. It stuns me."

"Actually, that would be four," Amy muttered softly.

Micah looked down at her. "Huh? Four what? Kids? Lucia, Natalia, Carlita. That's three."

Patting her stomach, she whispered, "Four."

For a moment, it didn't register. She waited. Ah, yes, there it was. He got it. His face went white, then red. His gaze shot to her stomach then back to the silly grin she knew was all over her face.

"Four?" he breathed.

"Uh-huh. I hope you're not terribly overwhelmed."

Tears welled into his eyes, this man who'd survived a horrendous experience and came out of it with his heart full of compassion for those who suffered unspeakable things. Micah pulled Amy to him, hugging her as though she were made of fragile glass. "Oh, no, not overwhelmed, over blessed." He closed his eyes and Amy heard him whisper, "Thank You, Jesus."

Amy knew there would be rough times ahead, crazy days and sleepless nights, but right now life was pretty perfect, in her opinion. She echoed her husband's prayer.

Thank You, Jesus.

Dear Reader,

I so hoped you enjoyed your trip to the Amazon. I've always been fascinated with the rain forest and loved doing all the research, creating the characters and watching them grow closer to each other and Christ. As I was writing this story, I didn't really have a theme. I just wrote the story God laid upon my heart, knowing he would reveal the theme in due time. Sure enough, after the manuscript was complete, (and still without a solid theme) I was having my quiet time when I came across this verse, Ephesians 6:14, "Stand firm then, with the belt of truth buckled around your waist." I had come up with the idea for the birthmark long before the completion of the story so when that was the verse for my quiet time the day after I finished the manuscript, I knew I had my theme . . . truth. I pra Micah and Amy are characters that touche your heart and brought you closer to the God of love.

Blessings,
Lynette

QUESTIONS FOR DISCUSSION

1. Amy is searching for meaning in her life, so she travels to Brazil looking for it. Has there ever been a time in your life that you felt empty, searching, and God led you to fulfillment through an unexpected event or adventure?

2. Micah, too, is searching for something. His memories, his God and answers to questions. Amy realizes who Micah is, but doesn't tell him right away. She's afraid of the repercussions she'll suffer as a result. Has fear ever held you back from doing something you know is the right thing to do? What happened?

3. Micah is self-conscious about his scars, worried about what Amy thinks of his physical appearance. She assures him his scars don't bother her. Is there a physic: imperfection that makes you sel

conscious? Amy tells Micah that God sees his heart, not his scars. What do you think?

4. Do you have a favorite scene in the story? If so, which one and why is it your favorite?

5. Amy has the intention to tell Micah his identity, yet she procrastinates, partly from selfish reasons and partly because Lucas told her to wait. But once Micah remembers and realizes Amy has known for a while who he is, he is understandably angry. Have you ever procrastinated doing something you know you should do and it backfired on you? What happened, and how did you make it right?

6. God spared Micah's life over and over again. He finally gives God credit for it and decides it wasn't just dumb luck that his assailant failed to kill him. Is there something you need to give God credit for? What?

7. Amy carries a lot of anger and guilt in her heart because of her mother's actions. When Micah approaches her about helping him find out if her mother has any knowledge about the attempts on his life,

Amy refuses to call the woman. Has there been an event in your life that has held you captive, unable to face it due to fear or anger? If so, what do you think will help you face your fears and let go of your anger?

8. Amy makes a pretty bad decision to go to Tefe by herself. She knows there is possible danger involved and yet she decides to go anyway, without making sure she is really well protected. As a result, she is almost killed. Have you ever made a bad decision that had a life-altering impact? What should you have done instead and what do you think the results of a different decision would have been?

9. What do you think about Anna's role in the events? Should she have tried harder to discourage Amy from going out on her own, especially into the jungle after Romero came down sick and couldn't escort her?

10. Micah feels torn between keeping everyone at the orphanage safe and leaving Amy alone to find her relatives. Have you eve felt torn between two right things to d but could only do one? How did

choose? What happened as a result?

11. Jonathas and Salvador both arrived at the orphanage under false pretenses. Jonathas took a situation and tried to do something good by watching out for Micah. Salvador wanted revenge. What do you think about these two characters, and could you relate to either of them?

12. Unfortunately, Salvador had his facts wrong about Micah being involved in his family's deaths. But he didn't find that out until after he was caught. How do you think he would have felt had he succeeded in killing Micah and/or Amy and then found out the truth? What does God say about revenge?

13. Amy and Micah turned a bad experience into good. They adopted a little girl that desperately needed a family. They offered help to the young man who'd tried to kill them. And Micah's life's work became helping victims of human trafficking. Have you ever had good come from a terrible experience because you stayed faithful and trusted in what God would do? Explain.

14. Do you think Salvador is redeemable? Can God still reach his heart?

ABOUT THE AUTHOR

Lynette Eason grew up in Greenville, SC. Her home church, Northgate Baptist, had a tremendous influence on her during her early years. She credits Christian parents and dedicated Sunday School teachers for her acceptance of Christ at the tender age of eight. Even as a young girl, she knew she wanted her life to reflect the love of Jesus.

Lynette attended The University of South Carolina in Columbia, SC, then moved to Spartanburg, SC, to attend Converse College where she obtained her masters degree in education. During this time, she met the boy next door, Jack Eason — and married him. Jack is the executive director of the Sound of Light Ministries. Lynette and Jack have two precious children, Lauryn and Will. She and Jack are members of New Life Baptist Fellowship Church in Boiling Springs, SC, where Jack serves as the wo ship leader and Lynette teaches Sunday School to the four- and five-year-olds.